Praise for *The Pit and No Other Stories*

"*The Pit, and No Other Stories* is a novella full of histories and ideas. It is a story about the trials and obstacles that fall into our path as we desperately try to unearth the genius within something we deeply care for. *The Pit* is a journey in it self, a ride with flashes of life and an ending in a place, in a world, you didn't anticipate but because of Rothacker's craftsmanship, you find yourself wholeheartedly accepting."

—Melissa Ximena Golebiowski, *As It Ought to Be Magazine*

"These tales are noir jewels born of a celestial meeting between Edgar Allan Poe, Jorge Luis Borges, and Alfred Hitchcock. Mysterious, cinematic, and dark, they draw you in from the first to the last. I read breathlessly to find out comes next, and in every case, what came next was a challenge to my own best guess. The superb, taut writing emits a vapor of menace and delight. About one of his clients' accent a private eye in an early story tells us, "It sounded more of a class than a geography." About these stories I feel almost the same—they are unique, in a class of their own, yet situated firmly in a geography bounded by the above-mentioned masters of suspense."

—Andrei Codrescu, author of *Whatever Gets You Through the Night: a Story of Sheherezade* and *The Posthuman Dada Guide: Tzara and Lenin Play Chess*

THE PIT

and no other stories

a micro-epic
by
Jordan A. Rothacker

Foreword by Everett Steele III
Afterword by John Reed

Denver, Colorado

Published in the United States by:
Spaceboy Books LLC
1627 Vine Street
Denver, CO 80206
www.readspaceboy.com

First edition: 2015 Black Hill Press
Second edition: 2022 Spaceboy Books LLC
ISBN: 978-1-951393-13-7

Dedicated to Jessica

The Pit, and No Other Stories

Author's Preface
Foreword by Everett Steele III

Table of Stories, Locations, Years

Afterword by John Reed

Preface

At this point I've published five books—four novels and one short story collection—and while the *Pit, and No Other Stories* was my first, it is still my wife's favorite. That matters to me. But for no reason should it matter to you. Why should it? Why should any of this? A novella from a recently shuttered small press and a little-known writer that sold only a few hundred copies and garnered maybe two reviews being reissued in a second edition by another small press when the writer is slightly less unknown? What's the con? Does this writer have nothing new to say? These are all valid questions, and your skepticism is warranted. The commercialism of art should always be viewed with skepticism, especially those efforts that blacken with the most cancerous elements of Kapitalism like *exploring new markets* with bonus materials, new editions, sequels, cross-product integration... gag... wretch... pray for death... ad nauseum...

THIS IS NOT THAT

This is about care. This is about perseverance. This is about rebirth and redemption. I love this book. It is the second I ever wrote, but the first to be published. This book made me an author (I have always been a writer). *The Pit, and No Other Stories* is an expression of unbridled creativity and economy. This is what it is to be a lazy perfectionist in book form. I call it a micro-epic since it scales big, but can be read in an hour. It is *Moby Dick* for the ADHD and twitter generations. And like Melville's masterpiece, it is about America, the idea more than the actual place. Fittingly, I started writing the very first story in the lobby of a very evil bank, the titular bank of this land, while waiting to contest overdraft fees. It was in that place I dreamed of a boy sneaking out of his house at night to visit a funereal pit, a small-town gothic. Years later it joined three more stories of very different styles and topics. I shared them together as a novel excerpt in Reginald McKnight's Narrative Fiction Seminar at the University of Georgia. McKnight was kind and supportive. Every student in the class hated it. A year later Andrei Codrescu was kind enough to publish the novel excerpt at his journal, *The Exquisite Corpse* (and he is even kinder to write the lovely blurb for this edition). Two years later the excerpt was enough for Black Hill Press, who only published novellas, to give me a contract for the whole book, which I owe to my friend and then editor William Brandon. The kicker was that they needed the book immediately. I asked for a month and wrote everything after chapter four in that time. It felt glorious. My wife read it and loved it and that's all I needed.

May you have the stars before the pit...

Jordan A. Rothacker
Athens, Georgia
11/12/21

Foreword

By Everett Steele, co-author of *Bon-Rappetit*

You are about to read *The Pit, and No Other Stories.* Reader, do not convince yourself that the title of this novel is a clever conceit. Do not prepare yourself to read a collection of stories about anything other than the Pit. This book is about the Pit, and nothing else. Judge this book by its cover.

I first met Dr. Jordan Rothacker many years ago when I was an undergraduate student at the University of Georgia. Rothacker was a young teaching assistant who had recently moved into our small college town to pursue his PhD, generally, and to write about the Pit, specifically. In the nearly twenty years since, Rothacker and I have grown close; our children often play together in one of our homes or a local bar while our partners sip drinks and talk about the world. We talk about the Pit.

I've read all the stories that Rothacker has released over the last decade. The subject matters range from the mundane to the arcane, from horny teenagers and their muscle cars to Jewish detectives navigating an apocalyptic Atlanta, but in the end, I'm not sure there are any stories that aren't about the Pit.

Maybe that's why I was so drawn into this book. It's one of a handful, three maybe, that I've read in one sitting, then flipped over and started again from the first page. It isn't that Rothacker is the only author to write about the Pit. In some ways, I think all stories are about the pit. Some are quite explicit, detailing a stock exchange or an Inquisition. Others are more subtle, their authors sending pages of stories into the world where they are discovered, or not, before drifting into the Pit.

This novella is sincere and satirical, science fiction and film noir, folktale and hagiography. It is a riveting exploration of storytelling and genre-bending. It is a void in which readers will see within themselves what lies at the bottom of the Pit, and how it got there.

The Pit and No Other Stories is about the pit, and no other stories.

1.

The Pit

(Pitt'sville, 1987)

Our town never needed a mortuary or a crematorium, we had the Pit; it was tradition. It was always out there, three miles north and west of the town center. It might not seem far enough for such a place, but you would have to know our town. The mountains have kept the border of the town pretty secure over the years. We have spread out a bit where we could, back towards the east and south—kinda like we were reaching out to greet or delay a visitor—but the western and northern borders have not changed. There is no easy way to get a road out that direction through the mountains and there are no big cities out that way to make bothering worth it to anybody. The earliest of our town settled with their backs safely against the mountains in this little, high valley.

When the name was changed to Pitt'sville, everyone had a different story of how the Council of Elders reached its decision. Publicly, the reason was even a sort of inside joke; to have pride in the Pit, "Pit Pride," was laughable. The Pit was nothing we ever advertised to ourselves, heaven forbid beyond our borders. All the other supposed reasons that made their ways around the very efficient gossip channels akin to small towns, ours being no exception, sounded to have a pretty solid kernel of truth. They were all still making their way around by my birth and were a part of my earliest civic education. Mostly, they were humorous and community self-deprecating, and I can still hear how sweetly my mother's younger voice could roll out the old joke of "Pitt'sville, because it's the Pits."

My main theory was that the naming choice involved the town's natural sense of isolation and secrecy and the idea of hiding in plain sight. If the town name has pit in it, but with a possessive and in a spelling like it was a name, it makes you think it is the town of a Mr. Pitt or some Pitt family, taking your mind and any discussion away from the presence of an actual pit. We refer to the men on the Town Council as Elders for a reason, they are the wisest men in town, and I can't imagine this theory didn't cross their minds at least once.

I have always thought a lot about the Pit. I'm just weird that way, I guess. Morbid, my teacher says, and I try to explain it off as just civic pride. It is our Pit, part of our town and its history, why should I not know about it? In school we have been learning our local history and recently studied how the Indians around here were mound-builders. Not here exactly, but not too far north of here in Pennsylvania and out in the western part of the state. Up in these mountains there is no real flat ground for building mounds, and why would you, you would just be imitating nature that already did that. We don't know too much about the Indians who lived right around here, but Mrs. Adena said that they used the Pit in the same way we do. It is a tradition old as time, she said, and the first Pitt'sville settlers learned from them when they got here. She never said where the Indians who were here went when the first white settlers came though. Adults like to leave things out, and keep secrets, maybe here more than other towns, but still how bad could it be? We have done other units on American History and learned how the white Europeans wiped out most of the Indians that were in the whole country. It's just another way adults control us, by not letting us in on certain things. They act like it's for our own good, but kids can handle more than they give us credit for. It's really just another source of power for them, as adults. I mean, it's my Pit too. I am a citizen, a child of Pitt'sville, and when I get old enough to leave, if I want to, I will do my part to protect it. And if I stay or leave and come back, I will have a Going Over just like everybody else, and hopefully one as nice as my Gramps had.

I guess my interest in the Pit has gotten worse since Gramps died. Actually it began before he died, when he got sick and came to stay with us. After dinner I would visit with him to say goodnight and he would rope me in to sad, winding talk about how his time was coming and he was going to that place, that place where his father went and his father's father. His mother and grandmother would be there too and the people before them that they talked about. He was talking about the Pit. Even in his fading condition, there in our basement, where he was sleeping on the foldout couch, he would look up and in its exact direction after a while of talking to me, as if it was calling to him. I don't know if he said it exactly, but there was the sense of it, like he felt he was going home. It's not so crazy, really. That's where we all go, where everyone went before him. I guess if it is where our families are then it is kind of our home.

It was in one of these after dinner talks that he showed me his watch. I had seen it before, but this night he made a big show out of it. It was a Hamilton from 1945, and he bought it new in Lancaster, Pennsylvania, taking the long way home from the war, he said. It was his lucky watch in the war, but a loaner from the service, so when he got out he bought one and wore it every day since. It had a little square dial at the bottom of the bigger square dial for seconds and the case was a faded golden color. It wore its age well, like my Gramps. He told me that he wanted me to have it after he went over. The idea of the exchange and Gramps having a last wish about me made me pretty sad at the time and I choked back tears and told him I would take good care of the watch. I mumbled something about how I would always wind it and clean it and never let it get scratched before he patted my back and tried to comfort me by saying, "I know you will, young man, I know you will." That night I could barely sleep. I was full of conflicting anxiety. Sad about my Gramps dying, but excited about what it meant for me, the watch, becoming a man, the Pit, Gramps going home. A week later he died.

So you see, I had already been thinking a lot about the Pit the whole time Gramps was here and then when he died, up we all went to Goodbye Landing for the Funerary Rites and Going Over and I got to see it close up for the first time since I was a kid when my Gramma went over. It was during the Rites, when they stood him up one last time so we could bow our heads in prayer before him, that I snuck one last peak at my Gramps and saw the watch on his wrist. His lucky Hamilton was going to go over with him. It's mine, I wanted to scream, but instead I just cried while everyone else prayed. I felt like such a baby, everyone so serious during the Rites, and I was just bawling, but they had no idea. And I couldn't tell them without interrupting the Rites or sounding like a spoiled brat. He had promised me the watch and I had promised him I would take care of it. He called me a "young man" and a man doesn't pout, not even a young one, so I stopped crying and kept it all in all the way back home and all during the Funerary Pot Luck, but I knew what I had to do.

All of that led me so naturally to this moment tonight, poised at my windowsill, about to go through. He went over with my watch and I wanted it back. That was the excuse I told myself. That was the excuse I would give if I were caught. The house was quiet and dark with sleep. The whole town was full and tired from celebrating Gramps. I just want the watch, Gramps promised; I practiced. And then I was through the window, out into the night. As we lived on the northwest side of downtown it was only two miles to Goodbye Landing, but this felt like the longest two miles I had ever walked. My heart beat crazily with excitement in my chest and with almost every step I paused to listen for anyone else about. I took this time to wipe my sweaty palms on my jeans before moving on. After what seemed like an hour, I was past the last of the houses in the northern neighborhood and moved a little faster over the last mile through the woods.

The moon was low and full right above the Pit when I crept out of the woods at last. I slouched up to Goodbye Landing, looking around me, frightened by how bright the night was. The moon, like a lid lifted from the Pit, got smaller as I walked up the hill onto the Landing. There it was, like a black pond. For the first time I faced it alone. I tiptoed out onto the landing and was able to see down into the Pit. Gramma, Gramps, their parents, everybody from Pitt'sville before was down there. The moon was far back now and its light could barely reach down into the Pit. It was the darkest blackest black I had ever seen, down in there. No sounds, no smells, no light, just deep and down. Standing there, sweating, breathing hard, looking down, I could feel the Pit calling to me, pulling me. It is my home. It is my future. It is where we are all going. Everything wants to be in there. I want to be in there.

What was I doing? Here I was at the edge of Goodbye Landing and I didn't know what to do. I came here for something. Yes, the watch. Gramps' watch, it was promised to me. It is down there with Gramps. I knelt and reached down into it. I stretched my arm as far as I could and hung my leg over to have a farther reach. I could barely see my fingertips so it couldn't be much farther. Gramps, the watch, it couldn't be much farther. I reached until I fell. And I was falling into the black. Oh no, I thought, I am Going Over, still alive and with no Rites. And down, down I fell forever.

2.

The Speckled Hen

(*New York City, 1959*)

I was looking out the window when I heard the knocking. It was a rainy day and the rain brought dissonant memories with its sound and appearance. The percussion of the rain, its rhythms on the cars and puddles, was so now and so cosmopolitan it sounded to me like the Jazz, the bop uptown. However, watching the rain sweep across the streets, when the wind took it, was more natural and wild, and reminded me of Beethoven's Seventh Symphony. My mind went back and forth in dissonance as I looked out the window like a ping-pong ball between a wigged composer and a black jazzman until the knocking interrupted with urgent rhythms of its own.

"Entre vous to you," I said with a sarcastic tough guy tone. I wasn't expecting anyone so if it was a prospective client they normally liked to hear some tough guy tones.

"Mr. Richard Winsome?"

"That's what it says on the door."

"You, sir, are a private investigator?"

"That's on the door too. It seems, Jeeves, that maybe you don't need me and the door will suffice."

"That is all quite humorous and I am glad that we can begin our business relationship on such a note of levity. My name is Quentin Craggswell the Third, and I would like to hire *you*, Mr. Winsome, personally, for a private investigation. Not your door."

He tried to make a joke and I almost gave him some consideration for it, but he seemed to be trying too hard. I let out a chuckle so he wouldn't hurt himself with any further efforts. He entered my office with a polite smile and a clean and innocuous beige manservant at his side. The servant dutifully drew out my guest chair for his boss while I took in the surprise guest of honor. He had an accent that was hard to place, but it sounded like money. It sounded more of a class than a geography. There was something hidden in the sound of his voice, maybe something eastern. It sounded worked, like the present tonal quality was not the ultimate goal, but had been reached with great

10

efforts and intention. The rest of him looked like a million bucks. Actually, he looked like a good solid ten large with the Savile Row tailored suit, silk tie, gold watch, and shoes of Italian leather that were probably cobbled by the tiny fingers of the Pope's very own immaculately conceived elves.

"I get thirty clams a day and expenses," I let him have the business as he sat down to business.

"Would you like to know the job, Mr. Winsome, or are you just that ready to get to work."

"What's the job?"

"We would like you to find a woman."

"I have found enough women to know I can do it, and I have found enough women to know I will need some serious specifics and persuading. And besides, who is the *we*? I didn't figure Marcel the monkey-man there to be your partner in personal business affairs."

That got a quick scowl and shameful down-turned eye out of the little guy in his fancy over-sized suit. He sat in the corner in my only other chair attending to an attaché almost half his size. I felt a little bad, but the tough guy tones sell the job.

"You will have to excuse me, it is solely *I* who am hiring you," he seemed unbothered by my shot at his monkey, "and though I represent greater concerns and

11

parties than the both of us, they shall be of no concern to you. This is mere personal business and this business is between you and I."

"Alrighty, Jeeves. Keep that collar cool. I'm just being wise."

"Well then, yes, of course. I would like you to find a woman."

"All clear on that. What's her name?"

"Names are of no consequence and unreliable in regards to this woman, they are easily changed. You might say she goes through them like handkerchiefs or suitors. She is often referred to as 'The Speckled Hen.'"

"Speckled Hen, huh? That is delightfully and deliciously drole, Mr. Craggswell, and I am sure it's a big hit where you come from, but in my line of work names are pretty damn useful. Do you perchance, Governor, have anything for me to go on, an address, social security number, blood type, shoe size, next of kin waiting outside?"

"None of that. However, we have no problem doubling your regular rate, and, of course, expenses, while offering you this as your *lead*."

He nodded with a little snap at his monkey who set to work in a mixed metaphor style like a bee, scampering to turn out my lights before opening his cherished attaché to extract a projector and two reel canisters. Once he got the reels threaded and ready, while his master and I sat in twiddling silence, he propped the projector up on his shoulder and propped himself up on my desk.

Now there was a film on my office wall where once there was just a water stain. As the lights focused, there was no longer a water stain, and no longer a film, but just a woman. She was tall and all done up, hair in a tight bun and a dress covering all the way from her shoulders to her knees except for a sharp cut out at the neck-line where it mattered. Even in black and white it was clear that she was a redhead, and freckles dotted all over her high cheekbones, forehead, neck, and arms, and I wondered where else they might lie. She was beautiful. If this was my only lead it was enough, because I was led. By the nose. Like a big, dumb bullock.

Otherwise, the film was nothing. It looked like a job interview. She was in a small office with one desk and one visible chair. It could be mine if my cleaning lady came more often than never. The woman in the film smiled and acted congenial. She spoke with no sound, but seemed to be answering questions about herself. She was not troubled, she was careful and intentional in her movements, standing from the chair and cruising like a grand, gorgeous ship around the chair towards the door. With her delicate freckled fingers on the doorknob she looked back towards the camera over her shoulder, maybe responding to one last question and that was when I saw it. She was leaving the room just in time and she was relieved to be at the door. Touching the door she had power, she knew it and showed it and she was ready to take it with her. That last look. The power in her eyes was beautiful and terrifying and I had to find her.

The projector was cut off and the lights cut on faster than you'd think a little guy like that could move. When I shut my eyes she was miraculously still there, but when I opened them unfortunately Craggswell was. I blinked again for a better view.

"Are you alright, Mr. Winsome?" he asked, but he knew the answer. His film was effective. I gave him a slight tough guy scowl.

"Well then," he placed a small leather bound book from his inside jacket pocket on the desk, "your first week of rate and expenditure is doubled and fit between the pages of this book along with a business card stating the telephone number and mailing address by which you can contact me as soon as the woman's whereabouts are confirmed. I hope it will not take you that long and the earlier this matter is settled the bigger will be your bonus."

He rose and went for the door, monkey man and attaché in tow. I picked up the book and fan-flipped the pages to confirm all the green. The title on the cover read *Field Guide to Birds of North America*.

"Jeeves? You sure there is nothing else that you can think of that might be of some help to me, something you are not telling me?"

"No, Mr. Winsome, you have everything you need. Just find The Speckled Hen."

*****

It was the least I ever had to go on, I thought. A nickname and a lingering image every time I shut my eyes. And the book. *Field Guide to Birds of North America*. Who stores and transports funds within the pages of a book, especially this one? Maybe the book is a bad joke on calling the bird a bird nickname? Maybe he had a stack of them around, the author is a family friend and a box of the books paid off a poker debt. No, the book couldn't be that random, Mr. Quentin Fancy Stiff-Britches Craggswell the Third did not operate that way. Nothing involved with Craggswell Industries operated that way. And nothing involved with Craggswell Industries seemed random these days. Especially not the recent merger of Craggswell Industries and Chrysalis International Aeronautics, hands joining across the pond the headline read, a limey and yank business unity not seen since the war. Front page of every paper just yesterday, and today, lo and behold, second in command Craggswell himself walks into my office to have me find some skirt. I can't imagine that he took me for such a fool that I wouldn't recognize the son of the man behind Craggswell Industries. Must have just assumed I knew him and thought like some good errand-boy chimp I would just believe this was a personal matter. Nothing going on here, ignore the name, the eccentric way of handling large sums of cash, just find my lost chippy, be a good boy now, run along with your book.

So now I was on the tail of a skirt, and ah, what a skirt indeed. I closed my eyes and there she was, alive in sweet, speckled cinnamon flesh. Found her, where is my bonus, Jeeves? Unfortunately, I opened my eyes to the rain through the window and she was gone. Where did I have to begin, and where did he expect me to begin? Did he think it was like some mobster movie and I could just walk down to the corner and flip a nickel to a newsboy and ask if he had seen the Speckled Hen? Maybe lean on the kid a little, take his over-sized newsboy cap and hold it above his head too high to reach and make him jump for it until he told me the Speckled Hen's address?

Sitting there, waxing fondly about my manhood in relation to newsboys, I started flipping through the book. *Field Guide to Birds of North America*. It was a nice old book; the last page read 1936 and told me it was published in New York. It was written by Dr. Fain Twigsley, no other name, just him all by himself, collecting information on all these birds apparently. There had to be a newer edition of this book since 1936, but for some reason I was holding this one, clearly the most logical conveyance for a wad of cash and a business card at young Craggswell's disposal.

No, I should live up to the title on the door for a minute, I thought, do a little detective work without even leaving my chair. The newsboy was safe for now. I counted the cash, five hundreds total, each evenly spaced in between pages. Actually very evenly spaced. The first bill was between page twenty and twenty-one and the second was between forty and forty-one and so forth three more times, ten individual pages in between, so twenty pages of text and bird pictures. And then the business card. It was all pretty orderly, actually, too orderly. Who counts out twenty pages exactly to put each bill in? I looked further, rechecked all the numbers and noticed the business card didn't fit. It was between pages 122 and 123, it was twenty-one pages after the last hundred dollar bill. Craggswell is an odd duck, I thought, and clearly the bird book was having an effect on me.

He was going to make me work for all these clams the old fashioned way, with my detective brain right here at my own desk. I asked myself, as he clearly wanted me to, what's so special about this page? What's he pointing to with the business card and how will it help me find the skirt, The Speckled Hen? The two pages had entries on three birds, the Ring-Necked Pheasant, the Ruffed Grouse, and the Spruce Grouse. I read all three a few times, it was all pretty straightforward, and pretty much the same except that the first two were from the Mid-Atlantic, according to their little maps, and the third wasn't, it was from more north, Maine and into Canada. The third also had a footnote tagged at the information about the female spruce grouse. It noted in tiny print at the bottom of the page that: "Though rare, the female can on occasion manifest as a speckled hen. One was observed personally in the environs of an unnamed West Virginia mountain town."

So that was it. The odd duck tipped me off through a bird book. And now I knew what I needed to do if I wanted to find the girl. I needed to find this Dr. Fain Twigsley—if that is his real name—and I needed to find that town.

3.

Father, Son, and Holy Ghost
(*Shanghai, November 1945*)

With the falling rain came the throbbing, a dull ache. Each step in each murky puddle, pain. More weight on the left foot, the right just the heel. Across the square he hobbles. No one cares to notice. Everyone is running in the rain. They run until the square is empty. He swings his right leg, bounding light off the heel, little pressure. The rain is thick in overlapping grids. His skin grows wet through his coat. Rising puddles touch his left toes cold. That one boot, far more worn than the other. There is no light, no stars, no moon. There is no sound, but rain.

Swei Li Quok halts his breath. He is listening. In the shelter of the overhang, he has a moment to pause. A wall of sound becomes no sound. He breathes. Crossing the square seemed once impossible. Now he looks ahead even further. The pain is where his right toes once were. He calls them his Phantom Barometers. He felt the rain thirty minutes before it fell. He looks down at the right boot. It is stuffed with a rag and tight to the water. Quok concentrates and wiggles nothing.

The wall is red. Around the corner, he sees nothing. He looks again. No light, only rain. He pivots back on his right heel. The heel is numb and strong. Eight years to callous. One bullet for five toes. His life for cowardice. Quok waits, looks and listens. It is impossible to hear footfall in this rain. It is impossible to see with no moon. Still, Quok waits for his mark, waiting for movement through the rain. He thinks of eight years of cowardice, eight years without honor. For a clean up sweep the soldiers returned. Quok played dead. Beneath his father and his friends he lay still and silent. He held his breath and held his tears. The soldiers spread blanket fire. Through the body of Quok's father one bullet reached his right foot. In the heat of August he lay, his sweat and their blood moving together. With night, Quok stole away. He was still in the hospital in December. It was there he heard the news. History in numbers. 80,000 Japanese soldiers in Nanking: his mother one of 20,000 women systematically raped; his brothers of the 200,000 killed.

21

From a door a man will come. In this direction he will walk. Quok will strike out from under his coat. He will stab the man in the abdomen and clutch the man to silence him. The man will fall dead in the street, dead in the rain. This is what Quok tells himself. He is doing this for China, for the Revolution. It is also for his family and his father. The man for whom he waits is not Japanese, but still he will kill for his family. Eight years, alone with his cowardice. Alone while the world warred, and to him it was nothing. The war has ended, but not to China. In his lifetime Swei Li Quok's father heard his son deny the Revolution. The Japanese came and Japanese went and now Swei Li Quok understands the Revolution.

Quok's father once stood here. Not geographic location, but thematic location. 1927 Peking, at a street corner, Quok's father stood. His eyes were across on a dark window. Sir John Waltzingcock walked down the lobby of the British Embassy. To his secretary Ms. Pool he said he was off to lunch. Jenny Kwan, translator and file clerk, was at the east window. Sir Waltzingcock directed his eyes to her ass. It was round in a modest black skirt. Jenny Kwan smiled over her right shoulder at the Lord and pulled the cord of the closed drapes. The light of the eastern sun filled the room, interrupting his gaze. Jenny Kwan continued to smile, Quok's father had his signal, and Sir Waltzingcock walked out the door. Two minutes later Waltzingcock lay dead in the street. Quok's father was gone.

Now Swei Li Quok must be his father's son. There is no one left. He pulls the dagger from his pocket. The dagger is dark in the shadow of his coat. Quok's eyes are used to the dark. He said he would do anything to help. They told him this would help. They had a tip. Across the street distant light is shadowed in the rain. The shadow takes a form and the form approaches. Quok crouches low, pivoting on his right heel. He holds his breath. The form is gyrating as it moves. This is the man, his mark. They told him the mark was a spasmodic-type. Quok exhales shortly and holds another breath. His right foot goes forward first. From it Quok steps with his left. The balance remaining on his right foot falls early off the missing toes. Swei Li Quok stumbles as he lunges, missing the form before him in the rain.

4.

Skinny Dipping With Land Sharks
(*Hollywood, 1982*)

"How could you even propose such a scheme. I told you my business is legitimate and suffers such slighting insinuations!" he yells with spit on the alliteration of the last sentence and slams the phone down onto the receiver. Snake-eyes green beneath caterpillar eyebrows black refocus in on the man in front of them, sitting six feet away across three feet of mahogany in a shark-skin suit, in an alligator and oak chair, a narrow broken line of shimmering gray cut into a deep finished scaly brown cushion.

"I'm sorry. Now where were we? Oh yes, Dirk. I hope you don't mind me calling you that." Slithering ahead, taking the lead.

"No, that's okay. Who was that on the telephone? Is everything okay." Ass shifting in his seat, wide eyes shifting in his skull. The skin of a sea predator making slight friction on another of a land monster. A tension is rubbed and stoked between the beasts.

"Nothing to worry about," calming, with a flick of the tongue and an easy smile, "nothing at all really, just the police, some routine matter, my name wound up on some list. Some shaken down informant must have pulled the name from the yellow pages."

"Alright, just as long as everything is alright, because I wouldn't want anything to not be... alright." He raises an eyebrow, an attempt at serious or matter-of-fact. Tweezed to linear perfection, the change in expression breaks the brow into a pyramid pointing skyward. Dirk's features are sharp and shiny and the calm assurance he tries to convey comes off false and amateurish.

"Oh yes, everything is um... alright," his smile spreads thin across his face like smoke, practically ear-hole to ear-hole, "actually better than alright. Pistolli, Dirk... Dirk Pistolli, I like that. You are a handsome man with fine, fine diction and I believe this part would be perfect for you. Normally, I say that an actor is perfect for a role, but here the role takes a back stage," pun intended, Dirk's sure, "to your presence as an actor.

This role would be happy to have you embody it, so to speak."

"Well, I will have to look at my schedule and talk to... my people, but," he was hooked, drawn in, flattery like the smell of blood, and he circles, waiting instinctually for his turn, "I think this project is something I can feel really good about. I will have to meet the director, of course."

"Oh, all of that will be arranged. Nothing to worry about here," he coils, contracted, ready, holds a beat, and strikes. "Actually, I hope you don't mind me saying, but the whole production has been waiting for you to get off its feet. Just put yourself in my hands and I will take care of everything. Trust me, after this you will be such a big fish, the whole world will surely seem like a small pond." The tongue slides out on the alliteration, a flick, and the snake-eyes warm and hone in.

"I am all yours," he smiles, but not without a little fear.

The fear is warranted. He is a fish out of water, and any fish out of water, no matter how big, will soon be unable to breathe.

5.

Skepticism

(Kansas, 1991)

The way it hovered over the wheat field made him squirm almost dirty-like in his seat. The cracked old leather with stuffing busting loose, molding and breaking further against his denim backside with his shifts and rubs. Those ants in those pants must have been slow moving ones, but they were active nonetheless. His feet lay still down there among the pedals and his hands gripped the wheel while that busted up old truck idled there straddling the double yellow where it screeched to a halt facing the wheat field just outside of town. He saw a UFO. And he was hypnotized. Locked in while it taunted him. Or at least he says he saw a UFO or something. Folks around here don't care to listen too much to what Ol' Hank Hemley says he thinks he sees or doesn't see. But this time I at least believe him, and that's why I'm telling his story. Now don't get me wrong I don't believe in UFO's or aliens from other planets, but I do believe that he saw something and something phenomenal, though even I might not yet understand exactly what it was.

I, unlike most of this piss-water town and environs that I happen to find myself in, went to college. It's only been a year since I returned from living with my uncle in Durham where I got my Associates Degree at Alamance Community College, but already I have made a reputation for myself here. The course I took on English composition is more than enough qualification to tell poor Ol' Hank's story. Anyway, my time at school was well spent and I developed a certain skepticism that isn't often found around the simple and mostly ignorant people of this community. This skepticism steers me clear of the usual voodoo mumbo jumbo and African-American mysticism some folks embarrass themselves believing in. I have studied science and some farm engineering and I have come to understand the way things happen based on cause and effect and other logical, intelligent concepts. I learned to look for the rational explanation for everything. I never even went to church before except when my ma dragged me.

I tried to use my college skepticism and easily dismiss everything Hank said to me, but he was so passionate, so convinced. It started that day he barged into my father's hardware store, of which I am Assistant Manager, all teary-eyed and exhausted and frustrated since he was going door to door trying to get someone to listen to him. So I listened to his whole story and eventually my rigid wall of disbelief gave way to a kind of awe. He did see something or he totally lost it for real this time. Hank came close some years back, about ten years actually, when his wife passed. At first there was a lot of sympathy his direction, but he became a real drunk, a real terrible friend of the devil, as folks around here say. And that drove his eldest daughter away. Out west to be a star, I guess, but then she just disappeared, fell off the face of the Earth for all we or Hank knows. And then Ol' Hank just grew cold, a cold silent drunk. He kept to himself, drove his truck just fine, and word was he could still fire a rifle straight and true, taking down squirrels as need be, Christ, he *was* a Marine once. Yet still, when he drove away from that wheat field that night he was different as if something really did happen. I listened to every word he said, actually hanging on each word, but not so much the words, since even though he was different,

Hank was still a drunk, but it was the way he said each word that drew me. Each frantic syllable had the keen affirmation of true Gospel and even though he said some outrageous things, that seemed to make it all the more true.

Well, enough of my prefacing. I shall now carry on the story of Ol' Hank Hemley as true as he, and now I, believe it to be. So, it was over the wheat field on the edge of town that Hank's eyes found themselves, locked in a gaze as the thing just hovered there glowing and pulsing, disappearing and reappearing, flitting about in any and every direction like a giant radioactive firefly...

6.

The Spasmodic-Type

(*Chicago, 1959*)

Chrysalis International Aerodynamics

———————— ConfidentialTranscript ————————

--They are bringing in a heavy hitter on this one. An old guy, used to kill during the war.

--Lots of people used to kill during the war. They were called soldiers. What makes this guy so different?

--Oh, this guy is very different from an ordinary soldier, or any soldier. He never actually served. But he is a trained professional, a killer. He would use the backdrop of war as a smoke screen to get to anyone. A real maestro. What better cover could you think of? He would go right into Hell, right behind enemy lines, to get one particular target. Crafty and fearless. Especially useful for counter-assassination. An assassin killer. That's how he made his name, they tell me. Oh, they would wax on about him on both sides back then. Everyone wanted him. Well-talked-about, for a man unknown. "He can see through chaos," they used to say about him. "Only chaos can see through chaos," they'd answer. That is how he got his code name: "The Spasmodic-Type." That and since he has no signature, it's part of the chaos. Each kill is totally different.

--That is all quite astounding, indeed. And disconcerting, nonetheless. I didn't realize this situation had gotten to such a level.

--Oh yes. And it seems they intend to take it all back down. They, like us, like things quiet. No, need things quiet, is more like it. British tidiness.

--Well, yes, of course, of course, the public can never know any of this. Who would that benefit? Publicity is an empty threat, it would hurt all and help no one.

--Exactly. There is a cold war on, in every industry, actually. Intelligence the greatest commodity, secrecy the greatest security. Especially at this time, for us.

--With the merger everything needs to go smoothly. There are many eyes upon us on both sides. Both governments, ours and theirs, and all the others, east and west, looking on. Everyone can guess at the implications at such a merger on the surface alone. Many must wonder if there is more than meets the eye, more than has been disclosed. We have already received some bad press for the German scientists we hired after the war, after the Air Force was done with them. We took that on the chin like sacrificial lambs while every other firm in our industry was doing the same.

--It's just common sense. If you want to get to the moon, you have to do your diligence, every stone overturned. Exhaust every avenue.

--And is this our next avenue?

--From what the Brits think this might be our last avenue. The last we will ever need. Tests on the first samples are like nothing they've ever seen and our scientists are in the process of confirming their data now, but it looks good. Very good.

--So we really need this heavy-hitter they are bringing in?

--The Brits, like us, don't like loose-ends. It is needed to tie them up neatly. So yes, we need this "Spasmodic-Type..."[1]

---

[1] Author's Note: It is always a tragedy the way legends begin and develop with no care for the damage they can do to real lives. The legend of a person can run away with the person regardless of who they really are or who they want to be. It is even sadder when the legend takes hold in an individual's youth; they are damned before they even have a chance to strike out on their own. The man referred to, quite sadly and pitiably, as "The Spasmodic-Type," was born without a name and had only various institutional designations before the unfortunate title was placed upon his muddled brow. By our contemporary medical science and greater skills of diagnostics, our unfortunate hero would probably be considered autistic, most likely of the Asperger's variety. His parents failed at their humanity when they left him on the doorstep of a Sacred Heart orphanage in Shanghai before they had a chance to encounter his biological misfortunes and acquire a second chance to fail at their humanity. The orphanages were quite busy in 1925 during the riots and strikes and it was after years of our hero's growth before any of the Sisters would take notice of his idiosyncrasies. It is easy for a child to be left alone and forgotten in an orphanage during waning British imperialism and growing communist insurrection, especially a child who didn't ask for much, and our sad hero wouldn't utter a word.

By 1932 he was taken off the hands of the Sisters and into the hands a man known as Le Cahier, as he was constantly scribbling and observing. He ran a privatized home and work program for difficult orphans on the outskirts of Shanghai, supposedly to source the textile mills. Instead, this colonial French Fagen molded the pitiable misfits he collected into killers and thieves. "The Spasmodic-Type," named by an English orphan in Le Cahier's care, was a difficult pupil to say the least, but Le Cahier was gifted in strategic thinking and found a way to work the boy, turn the boy's disabilities into dangerous abilities.

By 1959 his reputation had run far away from its original source. He is more pawn than "heavy-hitter." The young assassin he killed in the rain in Shanghai was less experienced than he, and overall unlucky. The coward had the chance to redeem himself, but "The Spasmodic-Type" came out on top. This poor hapless orphan has actually been the victim of a strange form of luck; one that keeps him alive and occasionally offers him his small pleasures while being chained to a sadistic servitude. Le Cahier operated the boy throughout the war and up through Mao's take over in 1949. After this hiccup of history, the operations were moved abroad, Europe and the Americas mostly.

How was a man of his condition able to pass about unnoticed in this country? Chock it up to basic American racism and xenophobia. He was trained to use the guise of East Asian tourist and anything spasmodic about him was just ignored by the general public as characteristic of his wily race. The man who trained him and made him the killer he became, this colonial French Fagen? Well, his story is even more fantastical than that of his sad pawn; but that is a tale for another day...

34

7.

Back/Away

(*Hollywood and Southwest, 1984*)

I saw her across the room, through the smoky fog of the party, like a dream of a promise that all the plastic people gyrating and posing around me could all just fade away into the air like the empty words they all spewed. Blonde hair, blue eyes, blonde hair, blue eyes, blonde hair, blue eyes, and fake tits, further than my eyes could bear. Until her. She was a brunette and her realness wasn't trite or dull in a city like this. And then her eyes: shimmering jade, shimmer shimmering jade. Eyes like primeval pools, and I wanted to dive into their murky depths. They were snake-eyes, but not like the eyes of a snake. Snake-eyes, like pools teeming with green serpents. There was a slippery darkness in her. I could tell. All from across the room.

I don't know, nor care, who I stepped on or elbowed or bowled-over to get to her. I couldn't even register if she was talking to or with anyone, but I wasn't, and I knew she shouldn't be. I walked right up and said to her:

"I hate it here. Let's leave."

She led the way out onto the balcony through the biggest fucking sliding glass door I'd ever seen.

Outside on the balcony I just stared at her. There was still some party around us, and I just stared wanting her to just go ahead and be who I wanted her to be. And she was.

"I'm Roxy," she said, and laughed at my heavy leer.

"I'm Cole."

"So where are you from, Cole," she said, pulling me into human interaction.

"I normally just say back east, but for you, I'm actually from West Virginia."

"Wait, your name is Cole and you're from West Virginia?"

"It's short for Colton. And it wasn't a coal town."

A waiter came with a tray and she took a glass of champagne. I took two and pounded both instantly. As she caught me putting the bottom of the second up, she caught up fast. She composed herself with a delicate, browned hand over her mouth for a burp, while I belched those pricey bubbles out hard over the balcony at the teeming glitter of LA down below.

"And who do you know at this party, Cole, or did you just crash it?" she asked, still laughing with admiration.

"I crashed here, the party happened around me without my desire or permission. The host is a friend of mine. My oldest friend actually."

"Two country boys in the big city? You both following LA dreams of stardom?"

"Dirk and I grew up together in a little town in the Allegheny Mountains, nothing to speak of, small, but not quite country. Anyway, after high school he came out here to act and I went to New York to write. Trite as shit, I know, all of it. Even triter was me coming out here after New York was a bust. The trite path of Fitzgerald, Nathanael West, Faulkner, except they were legit and needed cash. I guess I said fuck legit, I need cash. Legit got my skull cracked open twice in the pit at CBGB's."

"So, your friend, Dirk, our host, is an actor," She said looking around, admiring the house and the view from the hills. "He's got to be doing well. Have I seen him in anything?"

A waiter came by with another tray and we both pounded three a piece, tipping back the flutes in rapid succession. We belched in harmony, our first duet, off the balcony. Everyone around us gave us the stupidest looks. I guess they were supposed to be disapproving.

"It's weird, he's got this place, clearly money, hell, he flew me out here; but I haven't seen him in anything. Not tv, movies, nothing. He says he's been getting a lot of corporate, industrial work. But I have no idea what that means. He seemed pretty sad and lonely when he called, I guess dealing with dipshits like this can be taxing, so I came on out." I waved at everyone around us like they were just a tittering gaggle of some annoying animal. They didn't like that, but they did give Roxy and I some extra breathing room.

"I've only been here a month. Got here right after the Olympics ended and I feel like I've seen everything there is to see. I barely see Dirk, he's always working, doing what I'm not sure, but it's all paid for and he just leaves cash around if I need any. It's good when I can see him though, one on one. We carry home with us, but it's these people I can't stand. Coked-out Miami Vice wannabes. Smoking grass and pretending like they understand Warren Zevon or like they know anything that's going on in the fucking world. Like they're tuned into some Southern California mysticism, living always fanatically, like they're in a cult. Most probably are. It continues to blow my mind since I've been out here that these people work in the industry that manufactures myths and yet they still buy all that shit hook, line, and sinker."

"It's true, I'm here with my friend Debbie. She's a friend of friends of Dirk's, I guess, or his agent, maybe, and all she talks about is being discovered. She would never think to try to discover herself. But there's nothing wrong with a little coke or weed."

She drew her compact from her purse. Open, it sparkled with tiny grains like diamonds. We both did a bump out of her pinky nail. Then she applied lip-gloss to her wide lips while my head was beginning to lift, hair follicles tingling. The magic sparkling grains were applied to her sticky lips. I wanted to go in for a kiss, but she stopped me with one finger. High, and more confused than dejected, I watched as she reached up into the fountain of crimped hair on her head and drew out a thick tight joint. She lit it and took a deep drag.

Our first kiss was a party. Lip-gloss, coke, and smoke. And tongues. And champagne. And the night. We didn't need anyone or anything else.

*

But then some one, who could only be Debbie, staggered over, her tits bursting forth from her Lycra top—she clearly needed to be discovered—and pushed into our shared world, shattering a dream with full-on Valley Girl speech.

"Oh my god, Roxy! Have you like tried this lobster? It's totally like from like fucking Maine! Can I have some coke?" It was so contrived and trite at the same time that it was hard to hold back a laugh. This was my life right now. Roxy just continued to play what I assumed was her constant role of caregiver and supportive friend. She tasted the lobster first, agreed that it was "so fucking good," and gave her friend a bump.

"Are you having fun, Debbie?" she asked, wiping the cocaine dust from her friend's glistening upper lip.

"To-ta-ly. You are so sweet. I love you. You are like my best friend. Oh my god! Wait! Sheila has a fucking PRODUCER in a bedroom upstairs. A FUCKING

40

PRODUCER! She said I could share. Oh my god, I've gotta go! Wanna come? You're not blonde—you know I've been telling you you should do something about that—but it's dark, it'll be cool."

"No, I'm okay this way. You have fun, babe," and she kissed both of Debbie's powder blue eyelids, gave her a big drag of the joint, and sent her on her way.

"What the hell are you doing here?" I asked in what to me was the most flattering way for such a flattering statement embedded in a question.

"My story's as trite as yours. I'm just Roxanne Hemley, from Kansas, and I tried to get as far the fuck away from home." She took a long, hard toke.

"Well, I'm Colton Stable, of West Virginia, it's good to meet another outcast and exile." I took the joint from her and dragged the smoke into my lungs, feeling the tingle, and letting my warm inner space be projected outward into the immediate world around me.

She smiled at me and moved in, laying her palm flat against my chest over my heart:

"I hate it here. Let's leave."

And we did. Cutting through the bullshit of the party like it wasn't even there, we were soon in my car and down through the canyon weaving through LA. It hit the ten and just kept going east. Past West Covina, her hand on my thigh, I took my eyes of the road and put them in her shimmering jade pools while we sung our first non-burped love duet:

"I hate it here. Let's leave."

And we did. We drove the rest of the night, saying nothing, feeling the wind and riding the ten.

*

She kept us energized through her compact pharmacy. Twice she applied the coke to her lip-glossed lips and went down on me as I drove. I'm not sure if I absorbed the drug that way, but I was sold on the process.

Back east we drove, back for both of us, away from LA, back, away.

She complained not once while I tested her, cassette after cassette, Black Flag, Bad Brains, Crass, The Misfits, The Voidoids, Cro-Mags, The Jabbers. She could hang, even with GG Allin singing. But what sold my soul deeper into her shimmering green pools, deeper than she took me in her mouth—and that was something special, my guess being that there wasn't much to do growing up in Kansas except train for

42

grown up life in LA—deeper than I could ever imagine after knowing someone for less than ten hours was her love for Zevon.

I had plugged in the cassette of the self-titled album and when we got to "Carmelita," we both bellowed out that junky's lament like the sweet, sick junkies in the song. She then hit me with trivia, like how Warren's father, Stumpy, was Mickey Cohen's best man at his wedding and how Warren studied with Stravinsky. She was making me miss LA a little, back there, from here, and through her, I was learning to see the city differently.

"I thought it was just a place where dreams rot and die," I said to her.

"You're right, but it is still a place of dreams."

*

With dawn, her eyes left me for longer spans and seemed to be captivated by the desert. I was seeing her in a new light, daylight, and smoked another joint alone as I took it in. I took long tokes between cigarettes and also took in the dust from the road with the windows down. I was happy to be driving, to feel free, and to

43

listen to her. She told crazy stories, all triggered by the desert.

"I think I just saw a desert Herbert," she said, fixated out the window.

"Herbert?"

"Yeah, here I guess they are prairie dogs. Back home they are groundhogs."

"Herberts?"

"It's from my little sister, Nina. We were little. She must've been like ten, I was fourteen. Yeah, fourteen, on a family roadtrip, my mother was still alive. We were silent and content, the good old Hemley family back in the salad days. My father, Hank, drove and my sister couldn't be pulled from the window if you tried. She loved the way the wheat waved in the wind. At some point, out of nowhere, she just shouted 'Herbert!' We were all freaked out a bit, and looked around but didn't see anyone. 'Herbert,' she shouted, and then my mom saw it. 'Are you talking about the groundhogs, sweetie?' And my Nina answered, 'His name is Herbert.'

"We told her that we were going pretty fast and he couldn't possibly keep up, there were clearly more than one. I saw one on my side of the road and said 'look another Herbert," and we all started spotting them, seeing the world now with child's eyes, cutting through

44

the wheat and bullshit, all just spotting Herberts. 'So many Herberts,' my sister giggled, and we were so happy."

Instantly Roxy wasn't happy any more. That one memory seemed to bring others with it and she kept her head turned away from me. I hadn't realized until this moment that I was actually inspired by her. I could write a book about her and a chapter or story could be called, "So Many Herberts."

*

"I can't wait until we fuck," she said out of nowhere.

"Oh, yeah," I said like an idiot, while she writhed. The desert was doing weird things to her, but I was intrigued.

"You'll like it. It feels so good inside of me," she was practically purring at this point.

"You say that like you know first hand," I teased.

"Oh, I do," she trailed off, looking out the window.

"It was right around here," she said. "Yeah. I'd come to study with a shaman, to do a vision quest. I'd heard he was a sham, a crook, but I had to know. I paid him my $300, and he took me out into the desert behind

45

this roadside bar that he worked at. I guess he bartended by day or moonlighted when not out in the moonlight with people like me. Well, out in the desert, like a mile back behind the bar, a walk that fucking felt like forever in the dark, we came upon this little dome. Like a mound. It was really a wood frame covered in old ratty blankets, I could see when we entered, but he said it was his sweat lodge. He had me strip before we entered. He stripped too, and we wrapped ourselves in blankets. Inside, the fire was already going and everything smelled like sage and armpit sweat. He said a lot of stuff that sounded sweet and kinda like crap about us being in a womb, and the Earth being our mother, and learning what my power animal was. And some stuff in Hopi or Navaho, I can't remember what he was, I don't know if I know the difference. Is there a difference?

"Any way, he had this tea for us to drink and we both did. It burned my lips, they instantly chapped, and then it burned everything inside me. He told me to hold it in as long as I could, but it had to be not more than fifteen minutes before I was vomiting in the corner. While I was vomiting it started to work, the ayahuasca, or whatever it was. I watched the black bile sparkle and pour from my mouth like stars from a pitcher in the sky. Next thing I knew, he was on me, and as we fucked we exchanged bodies. That's how I knew he was a for-real shaman. I saw myself out of his eyes. I felt his little dick throb from me as my own and I pounded it into her, me. It felt good, I felt good, it felt really good."

The story just ended there as she looked out the window at the hard sheet of red desert. She had one leg crossed over the other, clenched, and I could tell she was enjoying her memories. I was coming down now from almost every drug in me and I was starting to see the woman next to me in the frightening raw. We smoked on a constant chain and she seemed to need a smoke after her story. She smiled at me through the haze and I felt a stabbing love in that smile that made me smile back.

What did I expect? She was the kind of woman who would like me. Who would leave a party with me. Who would leave a city, a state, a life with me. A woman who would instantly love me and want to fuck me. She was a woman who would take my stupid punk anger for truth instead of sadness. A sadness over my lost youth, since I spent my whole childhood dreaming of growing up and getting away from there. But to her my front was an appetizer. And she was the most frightening and real woman I'd ever met. She was perfect.

47

"Did you ever learn your power animal?" I asked.

"Yes. I fucked her," she said.

And I was in love.

*

We pulled off the highway low on gas, looking, with no good prospects, but kept driving, and soon enough we had stopped seeing desert; it had become something else. Scrub, brush, lowlands, and then really something else. It wasn't desert, it was just dirt. But there were buildings in the distance.

The sign at the city limits read:

No Haven

Pop. X Elev. Low

And it was followed by a less official looking sign:

Hey You, Don't let the Sun Go Down On You

We continued on slowly, rolling into the enclosure of rundown buildings, and felt unseen eyes on us. It was more than a town, no, less than a town. It was a cluster of fear and it reminded me of home. She swatted frantically at me, at the steering wheel, and I stopped on a dime as she opened her door. She leaned her head out and vomited right in front of the sheriff's station. The fear was too much for her—no matter how tough she was—it cut right into her, and she was trying to get it out. I was ok. This kind of fear was my pedigree. The old stained brick walls, of each plain square building, seemed to ooze fear like it was intentionally placed there. But if this town was staged in any way it was a success that Hollywood could only dream of. The dirt, the stench, and the fear were real.

I got out of the car, grabbing some napkins from the road-food trash in the back, and went around to her. Roxy was quick to recover and dabbed at her mouth. She tried to smile at me, but there were instincts behind her eyes, like those of an animal, that could not relax. No one came out of the sheriff's building to check on her or see who the hell we were. The building looked closed with no intention of ever opening. The only other sign we could see in this sad grouping of buildings, which seemed to be sinking into the dirty ground, was directly across from us, and it was a half blinking neon reading Pabst Blue Ribbon.

"Well, I could use a drink, how about you?" she said, and I couldn't tell if she was just this tough or really good at faking it.

"Once more into the breach, or the belly of the beast..." my metaphors and references were getting convoluted.

I put safety before chivalry and walked in before her. The door shut before she could enter, but it's okay, I was instantly knocked back out through the door onto my ass on the dirt road.

Behind me came a big, fucking, skinhead-looking asshole who hits quicker than you can draw a breath. He stood over me, but before he could do anything more Roxy pulled a straight razor from her right boot and whipped it open. She went right in and sliced the big fucker across the calf. He dropped hard like a stone, and with her other hand she helped me up.

We ran around the back of the building and caught our breath for a second.

"What the fuck was that," I asked her, more proud and excited than shocked.

"My father was a Marine. He was once pretty tough. He taught me that if ever the hairs on the back of my neck stand up to clench my fist and check my six. It was practically a jingle of my childhood."

"And the razor?"

"I've been in L.A. longer than you."

I kissed her hard and quick and we started running again, sounds and clamor rising up from within the bar and pouring forth from it in our direction. We ran through the dirt, through brush, then thick high scrub like a messy sickly forest, the sound of that angry menace of a town right behind us. And then, bam, we ran right out through the edge of scrub and slid down with crumbling dirt, down into a pit. My first instinct was to freak out. "Was I Going Over? It's not my time, the Rites haven't been read," instinctually flashed through my mind, but we landed pretty fast on our feet in this shallow hole.

Before us was an insane vision. Roxy held my hand tight as we faced it in silence. The angry menace had abated. All there was was a slick, shimmering, circular ship sticking half out of the ground. It looked like a UFO, and even though this hole had been dug to free it, its exposed surfaces were perfectly clean and shimmery like mercury. At a constant state of flux before our eyes, we couldn't look away. We squeezed hands tighter and they dripped mutual sweat. The shimmering, hypnotic vision got me hard and I could feel her getting hot next to me. Peripherally, I noticed the people walking up to the edges of the hole and out from behind the ship in jump suits like DEVO, masked like the government scientist spacesuits from E.T., but I couldn't move my focus. Roxy and I had started rubbing against each other, first just shoulders, then clawing at each other and our clothes, never looking away from the shimmering ship. Like mercury, like liquid metal quicksilver. It was life, it was desire, pure lust, and energy. I put her on her knees and took her from behind so we could both look at it as we fucked. Oh *it*, there before us.

I knew peripherally the spacesuit people were watching us and moving in closer toward us. They had instruments, like long rifles hooked up to scuba tanks, fixed on us, but I couldn't stop, we couldn't stop. We had to feed our eyes on the shimmer and feed our bodies on each other. Thoughts of LA, of how we met, of bittersweet Zevon loves and lives, seemed so far away, so far back there, so far away, back, away, and I cried hard tears and mouthed out to Roxy, "back, away, back, away," and she continued to back onto me, and I couldn't move away. I could feel the flames strike me from behind, engulf me, and I didn't care. I had her, she was on me, her torn panties aflame, and I could hear us both screaming, and the screams were not pain, but out of love and devotion to the beauty before us.

8.

The Legend of Amadou Quentin Diop, *Bismillah*

(*West Africa and Coastal Georgia, 1812-1836*)

Good evening. I am deeply honored, especially as a white Christian, to be here with you tonight, telling the story of Amadou Diop. He was just another man for a time in America, just another black man of sub-Saharan African descent in a time period where he was viewed as property to be bought and sold by white men, men like myself. I cannot imagine who or how I would have been if I lived during Diop's time period. I would like to imagine that I would have been an abolitionist, certain no John Brown, but maybe someone of some righteous fortitude. I have never showed much courage publically, but I have always quietly stood by what I believe. Any small contribution I have made to the world through scholarship has involved researching and writing about figures like Amadou Diop, figures who themselves have made great, but unknown contributions to America, a country that gave no care for their personhood and little to no credit for their contributions where credit was due. Every life has meaning and beauty to it, and the bare life of the African slave in America contained untold depths that should be told. It is true, that not all lives were as unique and adventurous as that of Amadou Diop, but his struggle and the forces that he faced were a common factor for millions of oppressed people. It is impossible to understand the greatness of America without understanding slavery. It was on the backs of the beaten that we built our might. This is the story of one man, that I have been able to piece together, and it is most likely more legend than truth, but it is often the legends told and retold that give hope to those in need.

Amadou Diop was born 1812, in southern Senegal, somewhere along the eastern end of the Casamance River. The exact location, which village, is hard to pinpoint, but we know that his grandfather was a griot. It was this grandfather who raised Amadou after his father left to seek work in Dakar for one last time and never returned. From his father's early returns, Amadou learned, along with his native Wolof, little bits of Portuguese, English, and of course French from a father who was himself a son of a griot and was raised to venerate communication. Amadou's grandfather was descended from a long line of griots, originally from Bamako in present day Mali. As he was of this tradition, he taught his grandchild not only stories local to Senegal, but also of the great Songhai and Malian Empires of which Senegal was at times a part.

We know that growing up Amadou received religious training in Islam from the local marabout in his village. He most likely learned a little Arabic, especially the first Surah, and other passages from the Qur'an and Hadith. This religious training was paired with the epic tales of his griot grandfather. Amadou was born lucky, fortunate really, and that theme will run through this story. There was a grace to him, or barakah, as his tradition has it. He was a large baby and grew up strong, standing over six feet tall by his fifteenth year (this we know this from the bill of purchase from his first official slaver). Due to his size and strength, his grandfather emphasized in the boy's upbringing the tales of Sundiata, or Son-Jara, the great Malian king who governed one of the most powerful empires in West Africa in the 13th Century. Sundiata is the buffalo and the lion, references embedded in his name.

A young Amadou learned how a young Sundiata was able to pull the giant baobab tree from the earth, roots and all, with his hands, as a gift for his mother. How Sundiata became a great hunter wielding a giant bow, and when he became the leader he united twelve kingdoms into one great empire ruled justly under the laws of Islam. Young Amadou also heard tales of another great and just leader, Askia Mohammed, of the Songhai Empire who made hajj to Mecca and established Timbuktu as one of the greatest centers for scholarship in the world. Physical strength, religious devotion, and scholarship were the building blocks of Amadou's childhood from his griot grandfather and the local marabout.

This picturesque Senegalese upbringing all came to a close in 1828 when Amadou, having passed the rites of passage into manhood journeyed to Dakar to find his father. Lost in the bustling port town, poor Amadou not only couldn't find his father, but was shanghaied into slavery. His kidnapper was a Taggart Fargrave, a notorious and proud man of evil nature, also referred to as "Taggart the Braggart." Fargrave was a pirate a century too late, but didn't let that hold him back. His crew was made up of Portuguese, Spanish, French, East Indians, West Indians, and even Chinese sailors, along with other Englishman like himself. They stole and sold whatever they could across the Atlantic. Amadou now knew captivity, chained in the ship's hold with dozens of other black Africans. The crossing was as horrible as we know that crossing always was for the slaves. We know that statistically fifteen percent of the enslaved died at sea. Amadou was lucky enough to survive to be sold.

Congress had banned the importation of slaves to the United States effective January, 1808, and yet this law wasn't always well-enforced, especially in the deep South. Taggart Fargrave sold what survived of his human stock in Savannah, Georgia on the not-too-secret illegal slave import market. Once owned stateside the slaves could be legally traded. Amadou and several others were transacted to the plantation of Thomas Spalding on Sapelo Island off the coast of Georgia further south. Spalding was a retired state senator of Georgia who at this point concentrated on agriculture, employing by some accounts 350 upward to 500 slaves in the service of growing Sea Island Cotton on Sapelo. Adjusting to life here for Amadou was very difficult.

Amadou Diop was of great physical strength and extremely intelligent. He was raised proud of these things in the images of Askia Mohammed and Sundiata. He was also devout and understood surrender or submission, but only to Allah, not to white men with whips and guns. He had a hard time holding his tongue and bowing his head, but watching how the other black slaves were treated he made his best effort. Soon he was to meet the man who would help keep him sane and safe from despair or an ill-fated violent response to his slavers.

The man was none other than Bilali Mohammet—and that is M O H A M M E T—in the antiquated spelling. Bilali was a much older slave, a devout Muslim who served as a sort of marabout for some of the slaves. Bilali died in 1857, and was supposedly born around 1770 in Guinea. He had been enslaved in this country a long time, and supposedly even helped defend it against the English in the War of 1812. Still he was in servitude, but of a high position due to his literacy. He found a kindred in Amadou and continued the young man's Islamic education, with an emphasis on West African Islamic law. When Bilali Mohammet passed away a thirteen-page document of this law written in Arabic in his own hand was found. It is now kept in the Hargrett Rare Books and Manuscripts Library at the University of Georgia. This document, like the lives of both Bilali and Amadou are examples of the secret history Islam has had in this country due to the slave trade.

Bilali was able to calm the spirit of Amadou, teaching him patience and pragmatism. With the regular counsel of a man like his grandfather or his marabout, Amadou was able to learn and study his fate, and the fate of his countrymen and women. Slavery was heinous, but it wasn't always hopeless. He discovered people in servitude with strong will and spirits. They found subtle ways of resistance in their daily lives. Sometimes there were actual acts of subterfuge, like breaking tools, slowing work against deadlines, slipping away from work, non-fatal poisons to slaver's food. The saddest acts of subterfuge, illustrating the hopelessness, involved infanticide (so a child wasn't born into slavery), suicide, or self-mutilation. The worst slavers returned these actions with fatal revenge, their honor—as if they actually knew what that word meant —in the face of treachery more important than the value of their human property.

Cultural resistance was particularly pleasing to him after being raised with such a background. Performing every day his ritual prayer, or salat, was forbidden, but that did not stop him. On some Fridays he was even able to perform the noon prayer with Bilali and occasionally others. The other slaves were from various locations down from Senegal all the way to Angola, and there were several different practices from their homes that they kept up in secret from the Spalding family and the other plantation foremen. He saw that many fought their oppressors internally, by never truly breaking, never losing their humanity.

Ultimately, it was Amadou's belief in justice, like that of the great Sundiata, that became a point of pride. He understood the whole system of slavery to be unjust, but plantation life had its own rules, the betrayal of which also irked him. Supposedly, he intervened when a fellow slave was being disciplined for an infraction he did not commit. Amadou could take it no more and rose up, his massive form moving before his better judgment and he struck a foreman. For this he was beaten and sold to the growing Retreat plantation on St. Simons Island thus ending his time in Sapelo and study with Bilali in 1835. Years later, during the Civil War, the Spalding home would be ransacked to ruins.

He and some other slaves were taken to St. Simons Island by boat, and as they came close, some of the other slaves who had been there before told Amadou a story that frightened them. There on the island, in Dunbar Creek, the spirits roamed angry, unburied. They were Igbo slaves brought over from present day Nigeria. When they had arrived here, they chose to jump overboard drowning themselves with their chain rather than be slaves on this island. Amadou felt no fear upon hearing this story. Those poor Igbo had their own victory and here he would too. The feeling and smell of the sea air on the boat must have been similar to that of freedom, and regardless of the beating, the thing that had risen up inside of Amadou was still on the rise.

Plantation life on St. Simons Island was no harder on Amadou than Sapelo. He even found the island quite beautiful. The marshes along the western side of the island took on a peach and salmon hue at sunset and when he worked near the eastern hard sand beaches he knew that beyond that horizon was home, Africa. On this island he worked at cotton and he worked at liberation. Later in life, Amadou would look back almost fondly to St. Simons Island as it was here that he made a plan towards freedom.

Over the single year he spent at Retreat Plantation under the King family, Amadou looked, listened, and asked subtle questions. He made secret maps of the island's shape and studied the tides. He learned about a small port town on the mainland, Brunswick, which was starting to see more and more visiting ships. And so it is told, that in the summer of 1836 Amadou Diop slipped out of his bunk at the Retreat Plantation in the center of the island, just one of almost five hundred black bodies kept like stock, and made his way out into the marshes and across the intercoastal waterway to the mainland.

This area would be described four decades later by Sidney Lanier in his poem, "The Marshes of Glynn," with its "shimmering band of sand-beach" that "fastens the fringe of marsh to the folds of land." The poem expresses the transitional nature of this type of geography and for our hero it held that same symbolic resonance. He passed through the marsh an escaped slave. An escaped African-American slave is the true embodiment of freedom since he has broken free from a place predicated on the lie of freedom. Only he understands freedom, for he has taken it with his own hands. In the "wildwood privacies" of the marsh, Amadou slept the next day, and in the "emerald twilight" he slipped through the town to the port. The first ship he found with a flag not of the United States was from England and bore the name, "The Shimmering Dusk." The ship was being loaded with replenishments for a voyage. Once everything was quiet Amadou went up the anchor line and on deck found a half empty barrel of wheat. He dumped the rest overboard and hid within.

In the morning he felt the roll of the sea, waves far from shore. Even in a barrel it was better than the Middle Passage of eight years ago; this barrel was his will. As the story goes, Amadou was eventually found that very first day, miles out at sea. The ship's captain believed in dealing with stowaways—especially obviously escaped slave stowaways—in only one way, sending them overboard and letting the sea decide their fate. The ship was owned by Forester Craggswell of Blackpool, a coastal town north of Liverpool. As we all know by now, he was the illegitimate son of a disinherited English lord. He was trying to buy his family line back into class through shrewd business machinations. Those opportunities were found in the Caribbean and often less than legal. As a shrewd man, he had also developed a skill for learning whom to trust. In this case, he trusted the captain and ruled in his favor. Before they could send Amadou Diop to an inevitable death, Craggswell's son Quentin spoke up. He swore to his father that he had purchased this slave in Brunswick, his first personal investment in the family business, some property of his own. The obviously simple slave took it upon himself to hide in a barrel, Quentin explained. Forester either believed his son or didn't care and declaring the matter ended, left the slave to his new master.

9.

The Eternal Return of Six-Fingers Willow Ptarmigan
(*The Woodlands, 180 BCE*)

They had come across the plains, chasing and being chased...
An ancient darkness... an evil that awaited the people here...
Fear itself... but food was still needed, still the hunt continued...
The hunt went in every direction... the people on the move...

These are the stories told. Her grandmother's grandmother lived on the flat plains of grasses. That grandmother's grandmother had a grandmother who only knew ice where the grasses no longer are. The Land gave challenges and solutions. The Land gave everything. With each story of darkness explaining the world, she could conjure light. As a shaman she shifted shapes, not just her own, but those around her. The darkness was real, as was the light she made from it.

In the morning's first light she packed up for her trip. It would take two days of walking and the ritual would be on the night of the second day. Her granddaughter, Deer Heart, didn't want her to go.

"Grandmother, stay. Who will protect us when you are gone?" said Deer Heart, focusing her wide doe-eyes. There were tears behind them. Her father had never returned from a hunt years before.

"Deer Heart, my dear little deer. I am going to a better place. It is a place that we will all go to." The girl had gotten too big to bounce on her knee so she had knelt down with her knees in the dirt to meet her eyes.

"You are special like me, though no one can see it. Whether I return or not, you will grow to lead. You have strength and you have heart." She hugged the girl tight.

Six-Fingers stood up and brushed the dirt from her knees. Deer Heart tried to continue hugging, gripping her legs and the bottom of her long buckskin. She rubbed her granddaughter's head and looked down into her big eyes. After compassion, the girl needed to see strength; that is what women provide.

"Your grandmother has to do what must be done. This is nothing to cry about. Your grandmother has a duty to you, to her people, to Our Great Mother. Now go and play and dispel all sadness. Every day is a victory. Grandmother is going to further victory." And with this she detached the girl and sent her off, a sweet pat at her bottom with her six-fingered hand as the girl ran to the other children playing at the tree line at the edge of the camp.

In trade and travels she had met family groups that would have abandoned her at birth for her condition. Her people believed that some times Our Mother gives more when necessary. In her family there was also tall Standing Elk and his strength and height had been put to great use. She was special and she had grown to prove it. Six-Fingers was the most powerful shaman in the woodlands. She could inhabit any form in Our Mother's land.

When she was packed up, laden and adorned with all the necessary items for the ritual, she headed off into the tree line saying not a word to anyone. Six-Fingers used a fiber cord to belt her buckskin at the waist. Attached to the cord at her lower back she wore the plumage of a female ruffed grouse. Deer Heart watched from the other side of the camp, the back of her grandmother, like a speckled hen, pass within the trees and out of sight.

Over the course of two days she wove her patterns high up the ridgeline. She took in the smells and feel of the trees, experiencing the red spruce, balsam fir, and mountain ash with her nostrils and the tips of all eleven of her fingers. The North Wind blessed her voyage, he was mild and on his wisps she smelled the animals in these mountains. In the evening of the second day she crossed blueberry thickets and after the last river, she ascended up into a flat high valley.

Knowing exactly where this was, she rested not long before so this last leg of the trip would be in one swift movement. She crossed the valley and took a trail up northwest out of the plateau. As Six-Fingers walked, she drew the antlers from her belting-cord and tied them tight into her hair. From under her buckskin collar she drew out first the necklace of freshwater pearls, then the mountain lion jawbone strung by a cord; both now on display as she walked up the path to greet Our Mother. When she got to the edge, she made a fire.

Now sitting at the Pit, she began the prayer to Our Mother, looking down into her womb. From her pouches she drew her pipe. It was carved out of steatite and shaped like a raven. Into the little bowl on the back between the raven's wings she packed the nicotiana rustica. The small fire she had prepared was arm's distance and she drew an ember to place on top of the tobacco. She let the smoke fill her lungs, but Six-Fingers would not vomit; the urge flashed and was gone. She had performed this ritual so many times before. As she let the smoke out she continued the prayer. The rhythmic chanting relaxed all of her muscles and her body shimmered with the tones and the rhythms. There was a powerful frenzy within the release and stillness. She could feel herself leaving her body and taking it with her. To greet Our Mother she became a bird.

Now a willow ptarmigan, she held wing around the mouth of the Pit, took a turn on wing and coasted down into the depths, cutting arcs in the air. Her wings were crisp white, movement of plumage and tendons so subtle, they looked still and stiff as they cut the air. No longer down, she was going up, up within the mound of Our Mother's belly. Up she sored and understood that this is where the brown bear comes from. From here the elk is born. Man, woman, and even stars in the sky are first born in the dark pool of Our Mother's belly. When the stars fall, they fall back in here. In here we return the brown bear and the elk. In here we return to be born again.

She flew up so deep within the mound, the highest, deepest mound, the belly of Our Mother. As she flew she rounded the walls, reading the scratches and edgings of a thousand violent births. The whole world had scraped its way out of here. With her tiny dark eyes she could read the history of the whole world. She marveled that the scrapes went in both directions and the deeper up she went the truer this was. The whole world, everyone, everything, man, woman, bear, elk, tree, mountain, and star have not only been birthed through here, but have already died and passed back into the womb tomb. Forever the world in both directions through Our Mother. The stories were wrong. There was no ancient evil; there was just the Pit. A lifetime between deaths, a brief flash of time outside the Pit. All that mattered was a moment of love for and from Deer Heart between deaths.

The willow ptarmigan ever ascended with no end in sight and so she wheeled and circled back down. For years maybe, the little bird, crisp white that she was, shielded her eyes from the truth the ripped and rocky walls told. When she reached the air of the opening at the bottom she sat on the edge and became Six-Fingers again.

She was not the first to find this place and this was not her first time here. It had been spoken of and travelers from wide shared stories. But it was she of her people who was brave enough to venture here. After her first return, some of the elders and warriors followed her back to view the high valley, but none would go yet to the Pit. Now that the ritual was performed, they will follow her back up here to settle in the high valley. The elk, deer, black bear, and turkey are plentiful in these high woodlands. The deep stream that runs southeast out of the valley down hill, in tiers and falls, draws the beaver and is thick with fish.

Deer Heart and the rest of her people will be up here in a week's time. Six-Fingers will only enter the Pit one last time, but it will not be for many years still.

10.

Pitt'sville Dot Com

(*Cyberspace, Today*)

We have made a protocol of controlling information. We are a shy town. We are a shy people. This does not mean we avert our eyes on the street and live a mirthless, puritanical existence silently going about our lives. Not even close. We, the people of Pitt'sville, are a community and amongst ourselves, in our community, we thrive in contact, joyous contact. We cannot pass one another on the street without a "how are you today, Mrs. Smith, I hope your husband is well," or a "how is little Sally doing, Mr. Johnson." Even something as simple as just the salutation, "good day to you," is said in every contact we have.

So it is best to make a clarification: amongst ourselves we are not shy, we are an open and happy community. Our shyness is only expressed in relation to the world beyond our little town. The shyness is not meant with any offense. We do not hate the outside world. We do not even fear the outside world. We just like our little community and our way of life so much we would rather just be left alone and continue living like we have always lived. Our geographic position is advantageous to that desire, but we do not have a gate, and though we do not advertise our location to the outside world, we do not actively prohibit entrance to visitors. We, the town and townspeople of Pitt'sville, sit peacefully in our high mountain valley going about our open and happy lives while the rest of the world goes about its own life. This is our tradition. It is not very old, but it is ours.

Our isolation has not led us to be behind the times though. We are right along with the rest of the world with learning and technology. That is what has made the job of controlling information more difficult. We acknowledge the outside world, and we experience it on our own terms through satellites, cable television, and internet. And as it gets more and more difficult every year to control information, it has given rise to jobs like ours here.

We Protocol Technicians work in eight-hour shifts, two at a time, twelve of us total in this position, here in the second highest house in the town. We have a wonderful view of both the town and the road to the Pit, which proves to be the biggest and most dangerous distraction to our job. Shifts must continue on schedule even when a Going Over is to transpire. The PTs scheduled can see the procession up the road out that window and it's hard feeling left out. However, our duty is a sacred one and we are proud to serve. For Goings Over of a close relation we have the ability to alter our schedules, there is certainly nothing inhuman or inconsiderate about our positions.

Our Council of Elders is quite wise and listens to the general consent and tenor of the town when making decisions (which is not difficult with a population as small as ours). Our Council is as open and honest with us as we all are with each other and there has never been cause to lie to ourselves. Maybe that is how honesty works, always in balance between a closed circle and what is beyond the borders of that circle. Control of information is not for our own sake, but to protect our shyness from the rest of the world. Our job in controlling information is quite difficult as it involves controlling the information the rest of the world gets about our town. We PTs are virtual nightwatchpersons and gate guards, ever vigilant and multi-dimensionally aware.

Sustaining our very precise and selective reality requires many checks and balances. We search every possible internet search engine on a constant round-the-clock basis, monitoring control of our town's name and representation. We have devised our own search algorithms to work in conjunction with and beyond those traditional commercial engines. With the satellite support from our considerate benefactors at Chrysalis Corp. we are able to further monitor and control information to our greatest advantage. Again, we are neither uppity, nor elitist; we are just very protective of our land and tradition. It is very encouraging that the Board of Directors at Chrysalis believe in this preservation of tradition and traditional values and was able so many years ago to find an amicable arrangement with our Council of Elders. If we had more to share with the world we would, we are neither unkind, nor covetous. Thankfully, Chrysalis allows us to safely share what we do have to give.

11.

The Pit

(Pitt'sville, 1987)

The boy woke furiously to a confusion of gasps and vomiting. It was he who was gasping and vomiting and each time that he sucked deeply in for air he retched out even deeper to expel everything from within himself. Both contrary actions were involuntary and the reflexes went back and forth, gasp and gag, gasp and gag. With each one was pain, but pain was a flowery white noise that ran all throughout his body. Every movement in every direction hurt. There was no end in sight to the pain, just bursting and rebursting flowers of pain all over his body and deep within his bruised lungs and burning stomach.

Gasping and retching, he also cried, and as he tried to wipe his tears and mouth with his cut up hands he just spread more blood and filth all over his face. More than anything, he was scared, scared all over and all the way through. A frantic panic fear ran through all of him and all of his actions. The blood on his hands and its taste in his mouth and sting in his eyes just kept the fear radiating.

His was now a world in shadows, brief flickers of light penetrating as deep down as he was. Had he slept till dawn or were the flickers from the moon? As his eyes adjusted—burning into adjustment—he noticed flickers around him, maybe beneath him. Through the chaos of horror and pain he thought of a documentary he had seen about deep-sea phosphorescence. Or maybe they were fireflies.

As the reality of the pain became familiar, deeper levels of conscious fear revealed themselves. He was in the Pit. No Rites, no Going Over ceremony, no death. But here he was. Was he dead? He could cry, and he did, and the tears stung his eyes with flares of pain as they shot back up to his surface.

He was in the Pit. And he was deep. The pain was beginning to be located. Burning lungs and throat. His knees, his arms, his right shoulder, and right side of his head all throbbed. Nothing felt broken. He could move his arms, turn his head, wiggle his legs a little. He couldn't lift his feet though. They were stuck. His toes wiggled on command, but his feet were stuck. Not just stuck, but he realized they were getting more stuck.

Through his mind flashed the only references he could muster to try to make sense of his situation. He was in an afterlife location for his religious tradition, and yet he wasn't dead. This was not lost on him deep down. However, his adolescent mind connected associatively to the giant trash compactor scene in the first Star Wars movie, and he even imagined briefly that something was swimming around by his feet. He could feel it. Was it his mind playing tricks? Or was it the phosphorescence; were they real? Deep-sea life in this deep, thick sea of human body stew. He also thought of the arcade game Dig Dug. If only he could dig laterally like that little guy, laterally and upward to freedom. The Atari game Pitfall came to mind next. He was in quicksand, but sinking slower than that Indiana Jones-styled adventurer. Slower, and worse.

These thoughts were his only brief peace. Trauma gave respite through playing in pop-culture, movies, games. His mind at ease began to move better. The Pit was wide, but still his hands searched in the dark. Instinctually, he was remembering his mission. His feet were stuck and sinking, but the rest of him could pivot. He could turn his feet a little in their new receptacles, but they weren't coming up or out. There was no grounding or anchor; it really was a muck of sludge, the worst sludge. Wheeling about in sinking, lashing frustration his hands eventually struck something more solid than all the other grossness they had encountered. It was his grandfather. He waited, and cried a moment, but to rest was to sink. To move was to sink too, but rest felt powerless. He wheeled back and put his hands on his grandfather's body. Touched his grandfather's nice suit jacket. A sleeve. He felt down it to the wrist. The watch was there.

His grandfather's skin was soft and like tracing paper. He didn't need to unbuckle it, it slid right off and he had no more tears left. The watch slipped easily on to his wrist, but touching a body he knew put everything else in context. He was sinking in a pit of dead bodies and the dead bodies were going to kill him.

In the flickers and flashes, the weird phosphorescence, he could make out shriveled skin of arms and legs making clothes look hollow. There hadn't been a Going Over for a while before his grandfather. He felt his environment without trying. He was down to his waist. He was poked by bones still rough. But others. What he could see, what he could feel.

Bones around him had become like marrow. Marrow was now a thin cream ooze. Where once was flesh was just a jelly, a clumpy jelly, with a broth between. And it all radiated heat. A green gassy haze hung over the surface of the muck. Ammonia, methane, hydrogen sulfide, propionic acid, these were the things that were burning and mulching up the boy's insides. His nervous system was breaking down, fluid filling his lungs, sputum up to the back of his throat, and he was slowly asphyxiating. And all around him, everything that pumped through or greased the organs of what comprises humanhood was now a thick surging bubbling stew. Gastric juice, lymph, blood, bile, urine, feces, undigested stomach contents, and minerals like potassium, calcium, phosphorus, magnesium, all sloughing off, with nitrogen increasing from the soil in the Pit walls. And that was just near the surface. Below, thousands of years deep, one could only image what it all had become.

A flicker-flash overhead. He ducked reflexively as best he could. Out of the corner of his eye he thought he saw a white bird swoop down by him; buzz his head. But no. But here again. Flicker-flash phosphorescence. It grazed his cheek and it was just out of reach. The muck was at his arm pits. He reached, but nothing. It looked like a piece of paper. In the fading glow he could make out the typed words "that sweet setter died in her arms."

Was someone dropping things, paper, into the Pit? Was someone up there? It was so far up, but he screamed and he screamed. The voice was in his mind. His voice. The Pit felt nothing, his voice was dead.

From the other direction as before, to the opposite direction—this time across his brow—another flicker-flash phosphorescence. It too looked like a piece of paper. So crisp. He wanted to cry, but instead just dribbled retch out of his mouth and down his chin with hoarse gasps. His ribs were closing in as the muck molded him to its form. His lungs were collapsing within them. He felt no hope and with each piece of paper he was losing his mind. The third one was close and in its glow he could make out one word, "Heraclitus."

His head was tipped back and as the muck overwhelmed his chin, his forearms, hands, nose and eyes were straight up. The Pit was devouring him, the bodies as one gelatinous mass taking him. The ammonia acid burn, tangy sour old blue cheese, a road-killed opossum, a stopped-up toilet, all and like nothing ever before. These were the associative memories of his final smells and sensations. And as he slipped further under, his fingers felt something and they clutched in response. His flickering eyes, now with no new incoming breath, darted back and forth across the sheet of glowing paper held tight in his hands hungry for anything with life. The last thing he read, experienced, before the rolling, undulating mass of flesh pudding made him one with itself were his own words, "Our town never needed a mortuary or a crematorium, we had the Pit; it was tradition."

The last thing to go under was the grandfather's watch, snagged on the boy's broken wrist.

12.

Dirk's Dead

(Hollywood, 1984)

Oh dear old damned Dirk, down and dumb and dead from the get go. He never had a chance.

See Dirk in his house in the hills. See his pacing by the south wall, a wall of window, more display than barrier. It lets the night fill the room. It looks out on a plane across the sky, the lights of L.A. down below reflected up above as stars in the dark, dead night. In the morning, both heavenly bodies will be gone, the soul of the city switched off and it's lesser reflection drowned in light. Dirk will be gone too, his soul, like the soul of this city, snapped off as his body hangs noosed from a stylish exposed beam in front of this grand window.

But see Dirk now, the last of him. See his pacing generated by cocaine, by Quaalude, by fear, by a constant stream of adrenaline that makes all of his glands throb.

Through the window, he is the show for the stars, and their reflection both. Trapped in between in his troubled terrarium. How did he get here? The replay, every time, more circuitous and serpentine, like the highways and off ramps down below.

An interview, a contract. An arraignment, a sentencing. Excited about the first two, ignorant about the dual proceeding subtexts. Dirk never questioned his fear or the reptilian sea-beast nature of his interviewer. Out here everything frightened Dirk, and everyone seemed kind of reptilian or primal aquatic. Everyone shined in the sun. A sheen through smog, thick with sunscreen or oil. Everyone seemed like they came out of the sea, a sea they would return to eventually. On verandas, café porches, by the pool or the ocean, they lazed like lizards in the sun, cold-blooded, needy. From nowhere West Virginia to a studio in East L.A., he entered this world through a language he didn't know (not a lot of outsiders in his hometown), gunshots in the night, and cock fights in the alleyway outside his bedroom window. He loved it and feared it all from the start, assuming like so many do that fear is inseparable from love. His childhood involved revering and fearing the ghastly as part of tradition and what better place to extend that pattern of belief than La La Land. A small-town show-pony turned big city pack-mule, a story as old as time. That was Dirk's story. A contract into bondage is what he signed.

See Dirk Pistolli, a professional actor now. See him move out of that studio straight into this house in the Hills. No growth, no progression, no striving beyond that first year of waiting tables and finding rejection in every audition. See him cashing checks now. See him buying clothes on Rodeo. Everything bespoke, making that perfect fit perfectly fit, bending his being to the will of the thread. Fashion win out. See the house fill with other people's tastes, now the loves of his life. So many loves, all for one life. See Dirk hobnobbing with the haves and not haves.

But the work, the craft? The meat of the actor's life to which he'd committed himself? Some commercials were performed and actually on tv, but always with dense costuming, and always for products manufactured by Chrysalis Corp or a subsidiary. He never understood the roles. They were all stage direction, but no motivation. Dirk's destiny had become dumb doggerel, like a dog barking at a crow. First name a dagger, last a firearm, and yet still he couldn't defend himself. They cut him down while using him, little by little, like pruning the letters from "asset" down to "ass." They made an ass of Dirk and signing that contract he assed himself as well. But lo, 'tis a shame he never played Bottom back in school.

See Dirk back at Pitt'sville High, in all the Shakespeare plays. The bard's words roll trippingly from his tongue. Sometimes they just tripped. His Lear laughable, his Coriolanus contemptible, but his Benedict, his Benedict was beautiful. Sweet Dirk was always a sweet soul. Too sweet for this world, most likely. Too sweet for this city, most assuredly. He taught himself to see Los Angeles as an other Eden, an island unto itself on the earth, surrounded by a sea of gold. He came from WS's world and fell victim to its similarities to our own. Like Othello, like Claudio, he was a victim to intentional villainy. Sweet Dirk never expected such things actually happened. An honest man—yet ironically a play actor—he looked false witness in the eye in dutiful trust. Destined for comedy, devoured by tragedy.

Even here, at this moment of reckoning, the lines flow off-book, "Spoken like an honest man who means not what he says," he shouts out through the glass and a city silent in reply or care. Tears fall as the sweet words cut against the complicated grain of his false tongue. Ever diligent Dirk, always off-book. Until a contract with doom, where the book was hidden and the role played him. He dreamt to be a vehicle for beautiful words. That is the heaven in opposition to a hell of corporate puppethood.

The last to see him alive will be his housekeeper, Naomi. See Naomi enter from stage left (L.A. night right). She asks him if he needs anything before she goes for the night, for the holiday. Asks if he is okay. He mutters and waves her off, hiding his tears. So many times she's seen him like this, so many more as of late. His body wound up on drugs and excess, she watched his life wind down. Damned, deviled Dirk, wound and down. She leaves him alone here at Christmas. Alone without his best friend, Colton Stable, missed and missing. Absent since September. Gone. Warmth of summer, warmth of his friendship. Gone together.

Dumped Dirk awoke that next day to the shards of another party, the shards of a broken day mid-begun, and awoke more alone than he had felt in a month's time. The absence of his friend was palpable. He was so alone, regardless of the starlets naked by his side. The energy Cole supplied had awoken in the home and life of Dirk something real, something deep, something missing. Something expressible only as love had found its way to the forefront of Dirk's consciousness. It had tingled the tips of his fingers and that morning they tingled no more. It was the pining for, and worrying over, his friend that sustained him these last months. But now it was clear that Colton was free from any stable. He would not have abandoned his friend, even if he left that night with and for a girl, as Dirk supposed the first few days. Back to New York, he supposed the next few weeks. Back to West Virginia, he supposed around Thanksgiving, but his family said the Stables were also in the dark. Dark-dwelling Dirk; dark Stables. If they knew nothing, it meant the Rites were never performed, Cole would never Go Over properly. And no matter how far Dirk had ventured from home, from tradition, this fact about his friend saddened him.

See Dirk save himself. One is more than zero and numbers count. Around his neck he slips the award, an afterlife-time achievement award, a retainer for services to be rendered. Get to heaven, Dirk, hell is no place for a soul as sweet as yours. Take the helm for once, and put it around your neck. Let there be truth in righteous release. You will have the stars before the Pit.

And there we have it—and him—hanging between sets of stars: true heavens above, and those reflected below on the black pool of LA.

Hero is dead.

13.

Dick Win Some, Dick Lose Some
(*Pitt'sville, 1959*)

I got up close to her at the train station. It was Podunk, West Virginia, and the end of the line, the last stop on the way to Pitt'sville. I watched her on the train the whole way from my car to hers, keeping my tail close, but not too close. I still had no idea what this was all about, but after what happened to her father, I was slipping into my big dumb protective act. I had found her. That was easy. Now she was leading me somewhere and I was following, since that somewhere seemed to be a big something for everyone involved.

At the station, only a few passengers disembarked, but several were boarding, each with small crowds to see them off. There was no risk in losing her, though. After a train ride of that length, gazing between cars, keeping tabs, I knew her shape well. I could dream in it.

Every curve, every dangerous curve, like the kind that require warning signs telling you to avoid at night, especially in a storm. Those are the kind I normally downshift towards, holding on tight, and try to handle. And she had them. She had a body that belonged on a nosecone. It made me want to fly a B-52 against the whole Luftwaffe.

Out at the curb, I kept my distance. Just another chump with no one to greet him at the station. Another chump waiting for a cab in a Podunk that didn't have them. My peripherals were on her, and I made sure not to check my watch at the same time as she did. After forty minutes she was done tapping her foot and looking in both directions between nervous cigarettes and gave up hope. Instead of heading back in the station to find a phone or some Podunk redcap-equivalent for information, she started out on foot, small overnight bag in hand, towards the intersection heading out of town. This was my move; a tail would be too conspicuous and impractical.

"Pardon me, Miss," I called in my sweet voice reserved for damsels and children, doing a little trot out across the street to her.

She looked at me as for the first time and I tried hard not to meet her eyes. I could still see them whenever I blinked and I couldn't let her feel my familiarity. She was off guard for just a moment and I had to follow through on the act while she was soft.

"I been waiting for a taxi-cab for the better part of an hour and its been a darn bust. But I just saw you hoofing it, heading in the same direction and wondered maybe you had a short cut up to the town." Oh, I was putting it on all golly gee shucks.

"You're going to Pitt'sville too?" she asked with a little bit of skepticism rising in her tone and perfectly plucked eyebrows. But my plan was working. Pitt'sville, that was the place.

"Well yes, Miss. How about that? Both of us going to the same place. Maybe we should walk together, these woods look kinda queer and it's bound to get dark soon. I'd hate to go it alone."

"I guess there's no harm in that. It's a free country and all," she said, but her skepticism had given over to suspicion. Maybe I was laying it on too thick.

We walked on a little bit up the hill in silence, me off to the side and a few feet back, a casual impersonal stroll. I've learned a little about trees in my time and was a little distracted from the Speckled Hen's gams and gait by the presence of red spruce, balsam fir, and mountain ash. This wilderness was as dense and dark as the city, but had a beauty that you couldn't find in Manhattan. Her orange dress with white floral patterns, which was a perfect off-shade contrast to her hair, and those stockings with the seam down the back could be found in Manhattan, but no one could wear them as well.

"So, fella, what business do you have in Pitt'sville," she asked, unable to handle the silence, and me over her shoulder stealing glances at gams in between tree appreciation.

Just then a truck tooted and rolled on up beside us. It was a blue, 1952 Ford, a fine specimen of human construction.

"You folks need a ride up to Pitt'sville?" was all the driver said, and we got in politely, with thank you's, but otherwise kept it just as terse as our host. I rode in the middle, still with the protective vibe. Our chauffer was one of those salt-of-the-earth, gentleman varieties, too stern and close to actual hard work to be a rube or mark. I pegged him at just a couple years under my approach to forty. He sized-up well, regardless of how little he had said. After a good half hour I gave up.

"That's a nice Hamilton you got there, mister. I had one like it in the service," and dammit, but my guard was slipping, getting sentimental.

"Thank you. I had one like it in the service too. Bought this one on the way home."

"It's strange, isn't it, what we get attached to?" I was bonding with a brother, but I'd be damned if at least half of my awareness wasn't on how close she was sitting, the heat of her thigh against mine. She looked out the window, maybe trying to ignore us, maybe just worried about her father and what she might find in the town.

The driver and I made the usual small talk of what company were you in, where were you stationed, all the familiarities of our generation. It went on for some time, since he was slow on the delivery and return. As we ascended some pretty steep hills, winding through the woodlands, the radio lost everything but static. I reached with my right hand to turn it off since he was keenly steering and with a curve rounding jostle, I smooshed up against her. There was little doubt she might think my shoulder-holstered sidearm was anything but what it was. I could feel her body stiffen and subtly shift closer to the door.

We crossed one final river, pulled up to a flat level, and out of the tree line the wonderland of Pitt'sville extended out before us. Norman Rockwell could not have exaggerated a quainter America than this. I felt like we drove into a Saturday Evening Post. The one road in led right into the downtown of shops with pristine white facades. Rows of houses surrounded the downtown continuing the orderly grid in every direction but the one we came from. This town was a lost paradise of the American Dream. But how? What could fuel or sustain such an embodiment of the Dream? I was waxing philosophical and I didn't care for it. The truck was slowing down, saving me from my thoughts.

"We don't get a lot of visitors here, so there's no hotel. There is a lady downtown right here, has a little café with a rooming house over it. I'm sure she has a room for the night for a nice couple like you." Our driver finally spoke again.

We thanked him kindly and got out. I got her small overnight bag from the back of the truck and I watched him call her ma'am with a real small town politeness. As he pulled away, we stood side by side waving and when he was gone she still stood right beside me. I seemed to frighten her now, most likely from the sidearm, and she acted like she was trapped, caught by me, a bird in my snare. She was still full of piss, vim, and spunk though, which I liked.

"So what're you doing here, in Pitt'sville, fella?" she asked, holding her composure and giving me a really hard eyebrow.

"Same thing as you. To try to figure out what's the rumpus with this place to make some powerful people hire a private investigator like me to find you when you and your father are mixed up in some secret about this place." It was time to shoot straight and I was glad that the jig was up. It seemed to relax her too.

"What's your name, tough guy. I never caught it?" she said.

"That makes swell sense, darling, I never threw it. It's Richard Winsome, or Dick." I tried to serve her up a little smile with that.

"Well, Dick, you don't seem very winsome to me. Kinda the opposite."

"Lady, there is an old expression, Dick win some, Dick lose some." I added an eyebrow to the smile.

"Well, well, that must probably be the most winsome you ever get. I should feel honored. All this trouble for me. But I've never heard that expression before. It can't be very old."

"Well, it's gotten old to me."

"And so, you're a private dick, named Dick?"

"Yeah, the most private type," and I winked and she blushed, pink roses bursting behind freckles.

"So how'd you find me and who hired you?" She tried to change the subject. Aw shucks.

"I snooped by the home of a Dr. Fain Twigsley. I saw a ticket for the train clipped to a photograph of you, as a kid, a ballet recital maybe. As for who hired me, let's talk off the street." And I was going to tell her. Jig up. After what happened to her father I gave up all client loyalty. That wasn't the kinda thing I liked getting mixed up in.

"You went to my father's house? Was he there?" She was excited and agitated and my heart was breaking.

"There wasn't a soul in the building." At least I didn't lie to her.

We went into the café. It was as pristine as the street and the buildings. There was a sweet old gal behind the counter. I let the pretty lady do all of the talking while I looked out the window out onto this eerily pretty town with eerily pretty people mulling about.

"Pardon me, Miss, the kind man in the blue truck gave us a ride into town and said you might have a room for us for the night."

98

"Why yes, that was sweet of him to send business my way. I'm Muriel. Just the one night?" It sounded more like a statement than a question, but my guard was raised.

"Yes, let's just say one for now. We're meeting someone tomorrow. My husband here will handle the matters of finance."

I walked over and handed the lady the amount she mentioned. Money mattered nothing to me, and Craggswell was certainly not going to see his retainer again.

When we got to the room, it was long over due, but I finally asked:

"So do I just call you, The Speckled Hen?"

"Ha!" she gave a hard chuckle. "I'd prefer if you don't. That's a nickname for my father only. I've always had these freckles. Call me Hadley. Mind if I freshen up?"

I left her alone and went downstairs to get a little casual information from Muriel. She was good for the lay of the land. Outside of the café, I had a smoke and waited for the Speckled Hadley Hen. I hadn't seen another person with a cigarette in the whole town and I felt a little guilty doing something normal that people in the normal world do all day long. Maybe they were all Quakers or Mormons? There was definitely something fishy about this place. It hid a secret, a secret someone wanted and was ready to kill over.

When Hadley joined me, looking as beautiful clean as she did with a glisten of perspiration, I could barely contain myself. I was now finally getting around to wondering about sleeping arrangements. It was a small room. One bed. And we had already lied about being married. But we could cross that bridge when we came to it. First we needed dinner.

We ate in the café, letting Muriel serve us up something wholesome. We made polite chitchat like a couple awkward sweet kids on a first date. To meet in person a dream that lived behind my eyes for the last few days should be a disappointment. She wasn't. Her voice was as hypnotic as her eyes and hips.

After dinner we went out and hit the town. The town looked like a white sheet cake for a wedding so we didn't hit it too hard. There wasn't much to it, just prettiness and people living their lives. Everyone greeted us cordially, doffing hats at my lady and myself. In the northwest corner of downtown a road led off behind a closed gate, this caught my eye.

"No wonder this town is so hard to get to, it's beautiful. They must be shy," she said in the moment and entranced.

"It seems like more than shyness to me. This town has a secret." We had been strolling with her arm in mine, and a shock went through her. It went through me too.

"I need a drink," she said.

"I checked with Muriel while you were freshening up, the town's dry. Unless we can find a speakeasy, some blind tiger slinging suds on the sly, I think our only hope is the bottle of rye in my bag back in the room." So that's where we headed.

She sat on the bed and I in the only chair. I was positioned by the window out onto the main strip of downtown so I could watch while we spoke. She slugged down whole the first glass of rye and I realized it was possible to like her more than I already had. She sipped at the second.

"So what makes you think your father will be here tomorrow?"

"Well, when he wasn't at the station I assumed he was here already. The fact that he missed the train yesterday can only mean that he would catch the next one. I can only hope that he will be here tomorrow evening. As this is the only rooming house I'm sure he'd look for me here. And now your turn. Time to be a less private dick, Dick. Who hired you," she said with boozy confidence. My favorite kind.

"I was hired by Mr. La-Dee-Da Fancy Pants Quentin Craggswell the Third himself."

"A-ha!" and she made her a-ha face. It was beautiful: steel-blue eyes wide, cheeks flush with rye. "That must be who father was scared of. Someone had offered him money for information about his town. Pitt'sville does have a secret and father has kept it. He had spent his whole life tramping all over this country recording habitations and migratory patterns of birds. He'd been here years ago, made friends here, and kept it on the hush hush. Recently, he made a discovery in the western part of Virginia, outside Lynchburg. He wasn't the only person to make this discovery either. It's a valuable and dangerous discovery and it led back to this town. My father is coming back to warn the people here, but since he wanted me to join him, I think he might be trying to hide me here. Of course, if you could find me, and its powerful people like Craggswell still looking, I don't feel very safe here..." and she started to choke up on some tears a bit. "No offense."

"None taken. I'm not touchy about the skills of my trade. But I am touchy about safety and crying broads." I left the chair and sat next to her on the bed so she could cry like a proper broad, on my shoulder. I was prepared to protect her, the horror I'd found her father in scared even me. This fear was almost cooling the heat her body produced in mine—almost. Her dress was orange and I wanted to peel every layer to get to the sweet fruit. She seemed to be picking up what I was putting down. Her jerky crying had turned to nuzzling. I kissed her forehead and she cooed as she nuzzled.

"I'm not going to let anything happen to you," I told her forehead sincerely.

"Well, I hope *something* could happen to me, with me," and she turned her head up for a kiss. I let her have it. She let me have it. I got to peel the orange, each layer, dress, slip, corset, stocking one, stocking two...

*****

I woke first from a brief nap, a nap we earned. I found my watch in the discard pile on the floor. It was midnight and the moon was high and full outside our window. Her hair was down and spread across the pillow. It had a golden glow in the moonlight. I kissed each one of her fingertips until she woke. I needed to snoop around, it was a hazard of the trade, and I didn't want to leave her alone.

She got up and I saw her by the window, the moon through the wispy shades, outlining her body. Dainty feet, thick womanly thighs, hips just as womanly, a bosom that would never stop bosoming, all pale in the light; speckled, dappled, and pink in all the right places. A sadness came over me, thicker at each layer of coverage while I watched her dress. At the last all that glorious red hair was piled back up on top of her head and pinned.

I told her my plan and we slipped silently down the stairs and out onto the quiet street. We held hands and walked in the direction of the moon, to the road that led northwest out of town, the gated road. I helped her over the gate, not that she needed it, her body was meant for movement, I just liked where my hands had to go to help her.

We found our way up the hill in the dark. Our palms were sweaty held together and I wondered why I couldn't just leave things well alone. Why couldn't we be back at the room, sweaty held together. I was getting nervous, another hazard of the trade. Dick win some, Dick lose some. That was the old expression, but it didn't need to be true.

"Look!" she gasped as the hill leveled out to a clearing. In the center was a giant hole. A dock, like you'd find at a lake extended out a bit over the giant hole. "What is it? What is it for? Why is there a dock?"

We got closer and confirmed that it wasn't a lake or pond, just a wide and deep hole in the ground. We stood on the landing and the full moon shown down only about twenty feet beneath us. We squeezed hands and couldn't look away, couldn't move. It was just a giant hole in the ground, but it was fascinating.

Suddenly, I caught something out the corner of my eye on the other side of the hole. I thought it was a Japanese tourist, white linen suit, panama hat, camera around his neck. He was all shaky and jumpy. Then gone. The moon was playing tricks on me.

"Did you see that?" I asked her as I drew my side arm and wheeled about.

"See what?" she asked with an intense fear in her voice. A fear that cut me since it was the only thing that made sense. I kept wheeling about. Where was he?

He was behind me, that's where. Then he was behind her and all I could do was watch as he cut her, cut her in as many places as me. I was powerless, couldn't lift an arm and my sidearm fell from my loose grip. My knees buckled and she gasped as we both crumpled. We held eyes the whole time. The guy was a real pro. I felt no pain and hoped she didn't either. Face to face we lay on the dock before he kicked us over the edge. My eyes would never close again, but always look into hers. Dick win some.

14.

Results

(Chicago, 1991) ·

Chrysalis Corp.

————————Confidential Transcript————————

--So?

--Yes, sir.

--Have you seen?

--I've read the report.

--Ah? Ah? And how about it? Favorable. All favorable. It works. The damn thing works.

--Yes, sir. But how does it work? Why does it work?

--I don't understand the technology, nor do I care. I care about results. Results are the only things that matter. Not the how or the why or even the damned who. Do you get that? Is this something you understand?

--Yes, sir. Of course. But you know I have to go back to the board with this. They are going to ask questions. Most people don't care just what's there on the page. They want to know the details. What went into creating those results.

--No, no, no. The board, like the stockholders, care about money. About getting fat and rich and then fatter. Thrusting their weight onto their wives until they're bored. Then their mistresses and secretaries. They are like all of our idiot customers for our commercial divisions. They buy what we tell them because it makes them happy, then happy we have convinced them that they want. It's the same with the board. When they ask questions you send them to that bottom line.

--But how... ?

--This is what we have always done. This is what you are here for. Their attention should be on that bottom line. It works. It damn well works. We have results. And nothing will stop us. The stars will literally be ours.

--Is it really that good?

--Good?!?!

--Yes, really that good...

--Ha. You sweet fool. These results are lost on you. But maybe if you understand better, you can help them understand less. Yes. It is really that good.

--Alright...

--Scotch? It's Macallan 25.

--Yes. Ok. Please. Thank you.

--Here. Alright. Yes, it's that good. Everything you've heard in the news of late. Everything in the rags that the poor slobs gobble up at the cash register. That's it. It's been working. The most recent prototype traversed the trans-Atlantic route in tests beyond expectations. It did the run in no time. From the facility in the north of Scotland to Kansas in a flash. Everything. Multi-directional hover and zero-to-what-have-you full-speed movements in any and all directions. The capabilities and market potential is like we've never seen. The town is ours, we have a deal with the Town Council, the Elders, they are called. We have secured the spring in western Virginia. We are ready to move ahead with production and the testing of other applications.

--And what about the crash site from '84?

--Oh that? Dead and buried. It was just another opportunity for results. Favorable tests, and a stepping stone to further results. We had it contained instantly. That's what diversification and synergy are all about. Our Hollywood division was on it. That division is in the business of creating reality. Professional actors, real life thugs, mercenaries, access to the technology from the other divisions. Diversification and synergy. The fuel was contained. Its power is extraordinary and its physiological effects can be quite disturbing in the raw. We safely salvaged what we could. And we burned and buried the rest. Back to the earth it returned. Huzzah.

--No loose ends?

--Diversification prevents loose ends. There is no failure, there is no collateral damage, there are only new markets. You went to business school, you know this. Everything shits. We have marketing people who turn shit into, "Wow, new shit! Get it before it runs out!" They sell our shit to the idiotic public and they microwave it for dinner. For us the focus shall remain on results.

--Yes, sir. I will convince the Board that all they need care and know—hiccup—know and care about are these results, these numbers—hiccup—this bottom line...

--How's that Macallan treating you?

--Good, sir. A little peaty... hic...

15.

Virology

(Arizona Bay, 2121)

Love is a virus, a parasite. This has been confirmed by all credible virologists, and all phases of science are moving ahead accordingly. The original findings earned Dr. Kinshasa Kirby the Nobel in Biology in 2029. The virus is passed from mother to child and has been so for millennia. Suspicions led to findings that were made clear from recent studies on test tube petri dish babies. What was once thought of as an emotional phenomenon or maybe even a metaphysical principle is merely a single-celled living organism that feeds on the central nervous system. Raw organic matter, fused and incubated in the Nativity Generator 29, gestated womb-free, emerged from the Generator with no capacity for love. It was quite clear from the "birth" of the Subjects, this difference from other humans. It is not to say that the children raised from this process were sociopaths or mentally or emotionally deficient. They could all believe in causality of actions and relate to other humans and animals with compassion and empathy. And as we now clearly understand, these things are not love. They are quite pragmatic impulses. On an individual basis, these Subjects could make no connection to another in any way once deemed love. We have seen that sexual intercourse, for the Subjects, is engaged in on the most primal, lust-filled level, but only after the most formal business negotiations, and at this point none of the Subjects have married. The lack of this virus is also marked by the incredibly strong immune system found in the Subjects. They are all resistant to all other viruses so far tested—with no cases of the common cold or flu—and apparently all bacterial-based diseases. Cancers and diseases of the heart or any other organ have appeared within only the smallest of cases, brief flashes barely documentable, and no fatalities so far. As we are in the 92nd year of monitoring the subjects, and as all of them remain at the pillar of health for their ages, we can finally document the purest interpretation of what it means to "die of old age." So far it seems that whenever one of the Subjects finally passes away it will be of no known specific diagnosis beyond the body breaking down from age and an inability to regenerate cells any longer. The children of female Subjects continue to be born without the virus and they will be monitored along the years of their growth and development.

We are still in the earliest stages of devising an anti-viral immunization for all "naturally-born" humans for here on out, but our hopes are high that this virus can be wiped out and we can all live with the length and quality of life of the Subjects. Our research has been swiftly moving ahead over the last few decades as the Subjects have donated generously to our efforts. They have all reached unprecedented heights of wealth for such a random sample of the population with little in common but the shared lack of a virus. Artists, engineers, scientists, CEOs of business—many here within this very corporation—the Subjects have been able to maximize the potential of human existence and time on this planet to live thoroughly and efficiently.

The trademarked fuel, that secret elixir from the earth, that the world thinks of now synonymously with Chrysalis Corp—*from cocoon to the stars*—is able to run our processors and every level of scientific experimentation and production at levels not even conceivable before. We will have the anti-virus mapped and in trials in a short amount of time. Our estimates are for months at the most. We believe that even with the anti-viral taken late in life, this once accepted condition can be eradicated from the human experience and we can all live better and more efficiently. This Fourth Industrial Revolution has been deeply organic and all the "softwear" and "zoe-tech," devised within these walls is making every aspect of life greater. Just think—as I'm sure you have before, in your positions—this rocket fuel can take life, but that is such an antiquated and limited view. It is ironically a clean energy source with a zero carbon footprint that will help slow the devastating climate change effects of the last century. It is also extending life and even giving better life. Science and nature have finally found a holistic circle. Life was once the key ingredient in death, and death is now the key ingredient in life. To think, it all just began with that fabled spring in western Virginia, and merger between companies, hands across the ocean, and here we have the future. It is our immediate possession. Soon enough the past will be in our possession as well, but I will save those surprises for the appropriate laboratory later.

Once again, welcome to the tour of Laboratory 23 of the Coastal Arizona Tech Complex of Chrysalis Corp. As board members you are getting all the most confidential access allowed for people of your position.

In this next laboratory, we are working in a different direction.

We have suspected for some time now that water has a consciousness. Just look what it has done here. It runs over and through this whole planet, through all of us. Now, over eighty percent of both. There is nothing else like it in the universe. It is understandable that aliens might come back for our water, we live on and are part of this enviable bubble orbiting around a star at that just right Goldilocks distance. As we have learned recently through the newest rocket technology made possible through Chrysalis Corp., the ancient scientists at Atlantis were the first to examine the marvel of water, but they cared too much, looked too deeply and their curiosity became their downfall. Their secrets are open to us now with the use of the rockets for deep-sea excavation, habitation, and experimentation. In some ways it is where we belong.

For nine months we each stew in a wet bubble, the nature of water talking to us, making us, and we burst with a pop into this world, another wet—but of thinner moisture—world. We have even been able to explore this phenomenon deeper with the help of the nativity generator.

Just look at that deceptively complex substance. As if we believe it is only two hydrogen atoms covalently bonded to a single oxygen atom. Smash it with a hammer. Burn it with your torches. It will prevail. Water always wins out. It is supple and cunning. When Heraclitus said you cannot step in a river twice he didn't realize it is because it won't let you. As we have seen in the last hundred years, the rising seas are coming for us, but we are prepared...

16.

Dick's Last Report

(New York City, 1959)

Report #:
4815

Date:
February 3rd, 1959

Location:
Apartment of Dr. Fain Twigsley, Ornithologist

Type of Assignment:
As per client request, locate redhead female presented on film reel known by several aliases, referred to by client as "The Speckled Hen."

Objective:
Locate, surveil, and question Dr. Fain Twigsley as to whereabouts of female known as "The Speckled Hen."

Confirm veracity of theory that in bird guide he is alluding to her whereabouts or a connection to a location in West Virginia involving a relationship between her and him. Confirm theory part two that client is more interested in the location than the female. Female might hold key to location.

Notes and Observations:
-Forced entry. Signs of disturbance in foyer. First room on left is study/office.

-Body of FT on floor.

-Signs of great struggle. Blood on floor, sofa, desk, walls, bookshelves.

-Blood pooling, not yet dry. Missed assailant by hours maybe.

-FT was messy. The assailant was messier. Possible psychotic. Possible sadist. Pleasure in the kill? Multiple stab wounds. Stabs and cuts.

-Birds. Birds everywhere. Taxidermy birds, every color, on book shelves, on desk. Queer birds.

-Open notebooks. Fountain pen on floor by body. FT disturbed at work.

-House empty. Untouched, but office.

-Objective assassination? Not information?

-I need my sidearm for this case.

Items of Relevance:
(1) Map of West Virginia. Circle over eastern mountains. Alleghenys. Pitt'sville dot at center.

(1) Map of Virginia, circle around a location, west of Lynchburg. Red ink notes by circle: "mouth of spring;" "water-source for birds;" "chickadees, glowing, flitting about on wings as of gossamer;" "origin? could it be? Pit?"

(3) Charts of water table for State of Virginia, Appalachian Mountains.

(4) Vials of soil samples.

(4) Vials of water samples.

(?) Stack of books on Ohio River Valley Indians. Lists of birds they ate. Ruffed grouse underlined.

(1) Train ticket for tomorrow. Pennsylvania Station to West Virginia. Clipped to picture frame on desk. Picture of freckled redhead teenage girl in tutu.

Note - Speckled Hen is FT's daughter. Miss Twigsley?

> Note - Did assailant see ticket?

> Note - Did assailant see anything?

(1) Short four line poem in open notebook on desk. Looks fresh. Last thing written? All about the birds. Poor Twigsley.

Sparrow on my sill,
At war with her shadow.
What victory can
Either
>> *ever*
>>> *have?*

17.

The Legend Continues, *Bismillah*
(*The Caribbean and Latin America, 1836-1848*)

Pardon me, where was I? Oh yes, Amadou Diop was now the property of Quentin Craggswell the First aboard "The Shimmering Dusk." In 1838 Quentin Craggswell was only a year younger than Amadou, and since he was an only child, many historians surmise that he took on the slave as a companion. During the first long stretch at sea, before the ship's next port in the Bahamas, Quentin and Amadou became fast friends. The former admitted to the latter that he had no desire to own him and that the latter could escape in Nassau if he saw fit. As appreciation for saving his life, Amadou made Quentin's name part of his own. They spent long nights sharing stories, Amadou learning about England, sailing, and the family business—which was all about diversity of interests and the scavenging remnants of triangle trade; while Quentin learned about the experience of slavery, the beauty and traditions of West Africa, and the religion of Islam. Quentin was impressed with Amadou's aptitude for languages employed his friend's skills in his own share of his father's business. They briefly docked in Nassau and when "The Shimmering Dusk" departed it was with the same number of occupants.

The second part of the life of Amadou Quentin Diop is from here on out a footnote in the adventures of others and large events of the mid-nineteenth century. Retelling his legend is like chasing a ghost through ships' logs, journals, diaries, letters, and biographies of the more famous people whom he encountered, or who encountered him. It is his relationship with the Craggswell family that is historically most important. We all know what the merger between Craggswell Industries and Chrysalis in 1959 resulted in for the already tremendous wealth of that family. And regardless of the business tactics and bevy of lawsuits and criminal charges levied at Chrysalis in the last half century since the merger, we must all admit that the mysterious rocket fuel, Chrysalis' central product, is serving as a sort of technological panacea for our age. It might help the effects of global warming be less irreversible. It has more than mitigated our dependence on fossil fuels. And there are so many other usages in experimental stages that are potentially improving our standards of life.

These benevolent applications of technology are in line with what we know about the first Quentin Craggswell, no matter the notorious and possibly criminal actions of his son and grandson. The initial good in the first Quentin resulted in saving the life of Amadou Diop, and his greater goodness resulted from saving that life.

After two years at sea, Forester Craggswell returned to England and diversified further into factories and coal mines around Blackpool and in Scotland. He left his son in charge of "The Shimmering Dusk" and the other merchant vessels they employed in the Caribbean. With his father gone, Quentin stopped even pretending to hide how free Amadou really was, or how integral he was to the business. Of this period, I like to picture Amadou Quentin Diop, a triumphant figure, strong in his faith and identity, performing his dawn salat at the bow of "The Shimmering Dusk" as it sailed east.

However, it was after a visit to Port-au-Prince, Haiti, seeing firsthand a black republic of former slaves, learning about the revolution, and getting captivated by the legendary figure of Toussaint Louverture, that something started to stir in Amadou. He was happy to help his friend in business and enjoy the wealth it brought them sailing about on the open seas, but he was feeling guilty being free while so many of his African brothers and sisters were still in bondage. It is from this point on that we are truly tracking a ghost. We know that Amadou had vowed never to set foot on U.S. soil, but he supported the abolitionist movement through financial aid with the permission and name of Quentin Craggswell. Through letters we can pick up the trail of Amadou in Brazil, Cuba, Puerto Rico, anywhere slavery was legal and he could help foment unrest and revolt. It is believed that he most likely died in 1848, fighting as a member of the St. Patrick Irish Battalion in Mexico City against the invading United States, a Muslim right alongside Catholic Irish, soldiers of various European ethnicities, and other escaped African-American slaves. In the last letter exchange we have of him with his benefactor, Quentin, an open-minded thinker and voracious reader, notes how he had turned his attention to the writing of Marx after news of the 1848 revolutions and strikes around Europe reached his attention. His father was managing factories and mines, but Quentin vowed to his friend that once he controlled the family business and fortune he would find avenues of energy and labor that are not demeaning, dangerous, or inhuman. There must be other sources for energy that are not dependent on human bodies. That was his promise, and most likely the last thing Amadou heard from his friend.

We can understand America through understanding stories like that of Amadou Quentin Diop. The African-American experience is the most important lens by which to understand America itself. Well, it and the even sadder and darker lens of the history of the First Nations. Though I do not practice his faith, and much of his story is legendary—and I can certainly never understand his experience as a black man—I have total admiration for Amadou Quentin Diop and will always consider him my hero.

18.

The Pit

(Pitt'sville, Outside of Time)

The Writer is at her desk with nothing, but a typewriter and an infinite stack of clean, crisp, white. She is overlooking the Pit, at a place once called Goodbye Landing, but long since abandoned. She is alone for miles and miles and years and years. There is the clacking sound of her typing and the sounds, like her gaze, are traveling out and down into the dark recesses of the Pit. The rows of words reach the bottom of the page and she draws it from the typewriter. Without looking, she lets it go. It flies, a thousand words without indention or punctuation about a dog she once owned that died in her arms, gone on a brief wind and then sucked down into the endless dark of the Pit. It will fall forever, never touch the ground, and never cease to be in the Pit. Another rectangular sheet of white is drawn from the stack and fed into the machine. This time she clacks out:

Time will end,
Space will end.
The Pit is only
As big as the World.

She forces the machine to force the margins and still her words only fill half the page. The page is drawn and set alight, like the last one, to hang on a brief wind before its dark descent. She keeps sending out the words and nothing ever changes. Maybe the fault is with her, or maybe with her words. Try as she might, they cannot become real. They are all pretentious, all alluding to something that does not exist, to something not real. The Pit keeps gobbling them up, one fake page after another, making them like they never were. But she remembers. And she knows that even the story of her dog, that sweet setter that died in her arms, that her mom bought for her eighth birthday, was not real. It was all a lie, art ex nihilo. Black shapes stab-clacked against, and in violation of, a rectangle of clean, pure white.

The Writer is at a point where there is nothing left. She stares out at a pit, a mere hole in the ground, and all her false words go into it, gone, but there is nothing of substance to fill it. All words and art fail at capturing life. All life fails at capturing itself, of having any meaning, of ever living up to any art.

The Pit is addition by subtraction; its existence is a deep, deep irony. The Pit is the mouth of Ouroboros and the world is the tail forever folding in. She knows all of this. It doesn't change anything.

Her ginger beauty, her American shame, her cracked actor, her detective, her punk poet, her sad assassin, her green-eyed lady, her love, her virus, all of these crisp white skins have molted and been shed out and down. The Writer's body is empty and bare; the Pit has taken it all. Her fingers tingle with all that is left.

She writes the last words she will write forever again and again:

No matter how far and high
Those rockets fly,
Everyone goes into the Pit.

From the Pit to the stars
To the Pit again...

Out from the machine, the crisp white flies, no longer clean, sullied with lies. The black stamped runes now indecipherable, out and down to the cold Pit.

Afterword

By John Reed

Hole

Easter Sunday. The kids had shed their stiff costumes and spilled into Riverside Park. A wide meadow, Spring green, crisp-cool, but with love enough in the warmth to welcome summer. Summer with its bright sun above the city, with its expeditions into the gray limestone of Upstate, and with its everything else in tumbling, no-school days.

Another parent was at my elbow, but I was alone in the instant, patting away a child who had returned to peel off the next layer—that sweater was not needed—as I marveled that this had happened again. Another season, another year. In the hills of grass, the children rode the infusion of new life like surfers, while I, and the parents, felt this subsuming, this becoming new again under the blue of the big family—the big family all and sundry and spinning in orbit—that had enfolded us.

If you know Riverside Park, you'll know the spot: I was under the tree at about 73rd street that looks over the down-and-up green that extends to 75th street, where the basketball courts give way to the Elephant Playground. On the downtown side of my tree: the dog run and the heavy stone arch to the Hudson Riverwalk.

I'd been in this spot before, under this tree before. All this magic, I had felt before. And I wondered, out of nowhere, as if the thought were put in me: how many pennies are lost in this field? And how long would it take me to find one if I looked? How much digging in this dark ground?

I'd written about holes before, their tendency, their desire to engulf everything, to mean everything. And stumbling into the life-keeps-going after that moment, I'd find myself taking up this meditation again. Jordan Rothacker's *The Pit, and No Other Stories*, is a wormhole of a novel—quantum in precision, and multiversal in scope. The realm of Rothacker's Pitt'sville is clear as a Maine day, but just beyond comprehension, teasing us, inviting us.

The Pit's eighteen entries comprise a kind of novella in stories—the crystals on the interior of a geode. A town, its generations, its mythology—and everything corkscrewing into the puncture of